BOSS UNDERCOVER

PART 1

J.S. BADHAM

Boss Undercover: Part 1

Copyright © 2018 by J.S. Badham.
All rights reserved.
First Print Edition: August 2018

Limitless Publishing, LLC
Kailua, HI 96734
www.limitlesspublishing.com

Formatting: Limitless Publishing

ISBN-13: 978-1-64034-421-1
ISBN-10: 1-64034-421-7

DEDICATION

Dedicated to my loving parents, family and friends. You never stopped believing in me.

CHAPTER ONE

ZACK

"When can I see you again?" A deep, sensuous purr left the back of her throat. She laid hidden beneath the duvet covers, twirling a single lock of hair between the pads of her finger and thumb. Her tender lips pursed together as she ran her painted nail across Zack's naked back, playfully drawing circles to tempt him back to bed.

He quivered gently, painfully distracted by her sensitive touch, yet he gritted his teeth and bent over to gather his discarded clothes from the floor.

He said nothing, allowing silence to linger within the room, a frustration to the stranger wrapped like a present in the bed and whose long sigh shook each corner of the room. It didn't receive any sympathy from Zack; he was more bravely concerned with slipping on his dark blue linen shirt, to escape his own nagging conscience, that hungered to tumble and twist back into the embrace of the sheets.

"Zack?"

Again, he made no effort to reply. He guessed she was disappointed from the sound of her gentle sigh.

She exhaled. "Zack?" Then she sat up, sliding her arms gradually around his neck, each inch of her body pressed up against him. It was driving him crazy.

"What?" he gently said, brushing her fingers away from his face; her persistence was beginning to bug him.

"I asked when I might be able to see you again." Her hot breath crept above the edges of his collar. "You could stay, you know?" she whispered, dangerously dropping a wet kiss below his ear lobe.

Zack turned, pitifully clasping both her hands, as he exhaled. "You know I come when I please. I don't like to trouble myself with *complications*, sweetheart. It was a one-night stand. End of." Then he let them loose, placing his own hands back in his trouser pockets.

"I hate hearing that," she confessed, a shower of red locks shimmering down onto her naked shoulders as she shook her head.

Zack shrugged loosely. "There's nothing more to say," he muttered, planting a stiff kiss onto the right side of her cheek.

Zack headed out from the bedroom towards the front door. From behind, he could hear the sudden scuttle of feet trying to keep up.

"Zack!" she called out breathlessly as she stopped short near the bottom of the staircase whilst anxiously tightening a black silk robe around her petite frame. Specks of last night's mascara clung beneath her eyes, her hair was static in places, and that plea within her expression should have beckoned him to stay.

But he did not reply. He left the apartment complex, the cold wind nipping on his bare cheeks, calming, slightly, the killing headache he felt moments before. He was also grateful she hadn't followed him out when he dared to look back. He was certain she got the memo.

His silver convertible sat on the opposite curb, just as he remembered.

It was ten in the morning. Several people wrapped up in scarves and hoodies were congregated around a car's boot, lifting off the bags of shopping stacked up near enough to the roof, some curiously watching Zack as he got into his fancy car, where he obnoxiously revved the engine. He was trying to leave an impression on the residents tucked up in their terraced housing all up and down the narrow road. Vanity made him gag at the sight of people carriers and two-door cars as he drove past them; it was something he'd never be caught dead in.

Zack switched off the radio, contemplating yesterday's disaster. It was supposed to have been a celebration of corporate businesses: the champagne flutes, the four-course cuisine, the enchanted small orchestra conducting a piece in the background, and the unlimited serving at the bar. Oh, it was all there, only Zack's appearance took the cherry off the top.

He was directed to a table full partly of wannabe Santas, greying, coarse-bearded, late middle-aged old men, blabbering on in their comical tones whilst toasting to their success. He was the youngest, sandwiched uncomfortably between two tall, plump men laughing hysterically and slamming their fists inappropriately at times on the surface, knocking the dishes and cutlery out of place. He could have also sworn darts of spit fell into his soup, as they talked around him as if he weren't there.

"I heard that!" Some fifty-year-old Asian gentleman howled with laughter. "Utter garbage!"

"Oh, who cares about renewability? The government thinks they can impose that on us!" one of the Santas agreed, laughing as he patted his egg-shaped belly.

That was when Zack's existence became known. He could remember meekly tuning in, opining his thoughts, and gathering a deadly look from each male representative. "I'm going to optimise it. You don't know the scale of profit to be made," he'd stated, confidently sitting up but anxiously turning a spoon between his fingers.

"Oh? Oh! Looks like we have a pansy here, gentlemen. All for green!" someone cackled on the right edge of the table.

"No, what keeps the world spinning is money-grabbing resources. Fossil fuels!"

"Hear! Hear!"

Laughter embraced the rest of the conversation, the clink of flutes kissing the brim of each glass and waiters and waitresses madly rushing around to collect or refill empty glasses, completely sucked dry by each participant around the table. Zack had barely finished his first.

"Oh! Oh! I know you!" someone perked up,

addressing Zack. "You're Elijah's son. Oh, that is a shame. Now, there's a man who knows how to run a company." He laughed. "And a party!"

"He runs Bensons?"

"That can't be right."

"I thought Elijah just wasn't coming tonight!"

And there was the madness. After running the company for a year and a half, he was still not recognised as its new leader; it was his father they'd crowned the haloed saviour of Bensons. It made that night so very uncomfortable that he transferred donations towards the charity gala without knowing what he was bidding for and left, hopping on over to the city central bars and clubs, hoping for a stiff drink. That's when he met *her.* He didn't know her name, just that she sat all alone on a stool at the bar, incessantly complaining about some ex to the bartender. So, like the knight in shining armour that he was, he swept her off her feet, ensuring the next few hours were the best goddamn moments of her life, and to erase the evening's terrible circumstances. It was just too bad she had the tendency throughout the night to open a floodgate of emotions, making it feel like an audition to match her ex than the meaningless sex he desired. *Bon Voyage!* He'd mentally crossed her name off the list.

It was frustrating that sex was beginning to feel mundane. He desired something different.

Zack took his car keys out of the ignition, the sound of the engine replaced by the empty silence of his garage. He was home. The pinnacle so far of this day. His home rested high above the city skyline, giving him full access to the animated scene below, a blissful thing knowing any ordinary coffee could suddenly be the world's best coffee when consumed on the outside balcony, high up on a hill.

He did not delay getting inside, dropping his blazer on the banister of the staircase as he made his way through to the central room, already craving a glass of liquor despite the madness of it being the early hours in the morning. Adjacent to the edge of the kitchen island counter, a glass display cabinet held Zack's prized treasures, several bottles ranging from whiskey to gin. It was like a taste of heaven as he felt the heavy liquid snake down his throat, erasing the irritable headache and offering a first-hand rejuvenation, of feeling refreshed and ready.

"A'ight, Zacky boy," a familiar voice said, intruding Zack's barely three-second peace. His feet shifted direction, his curiosity soon deflating at the sight of his friend, Kyle, exiting the exclusive penthouse lift at the bottom of the long hallway. He was a sight for sore eyes. Whatever made him decide to wear bright red chinos and a cream fedora didn't surprise Zack.

"How did you get in?" Zack asked, disinterested to even ask about Kyle's stylistic choices. He placed his empty whiskey glass onto the counter. Kyle entered the central room, his vibrant red chinos pulling focus. It had this simple grandeur, cream walls, black marble floor skirting, and large white, leather snaking sofas either side, leaving a contemporary feel.

Kyle smirked, his faint freckles tugging along

with it. "I fucked your maid and she slipped the access key to the lift."

"Well, shit. At least you're getting some better action," Zack said, shaking his head as he returned to his empty glass and poured another drop.

"What's got your knickers in a twist?" Kyle snickered, sitting down on the sofa and resting one leg casually over the other.

"Don't even ask."

"So, what? Shit event? Shit hook-up?" Kyle suggested, his smugness evident from the raised blondish eyebrow halfway up his forehead.

"Both," he replied earnestly, sighing as he sat down on the opposite sofa and kicked up his feet onto the glass coffee table.

"Why? First, obviously, starting with the sex part."

Zack rolled his eyes. "Of course, that would be your first concern." Consciously swirling the light brown liquid around in the glass, he explained, "It wasn't bad. It just wasn't great. Where is she?"

"Who?"

"That mystery woman who will barge into my life and actually make me painfully hard again," Zack muttered, swirling the liquid once more around in his glass.

"Well, we could always set you up on Grindr," Kyle sneered, slapping his hand on his ankle.

"Fuck off," Zack spat, flopping back into the sofa.

"Oh. Yeah. I forgot," Kyle said. He began dishing into his leather jacket as he took out his phone. Zack raised his head up slightly, peering through slitted eyes before flopping back in disinterest.

"Here, check this out," Kyle said, throwing his phone casually over to him. Zack grumbled incoherently as he took Kyle's phone into his hands.

"Neil Barracks writes that Zack Benson has 'no potential to expand and runs the company like an amateur. Better yet…does he even exist? I don't think anyone has even heard of him. Does Bensons Corporations need to go back to Nursey for some brush-up on its management?'" Zack read out aloud before tossing the phone onto the side of the sofa.

"Hey, hey. There's still more to read," Kyle insisted. "This guy has got the hound dogs on you!" He played incessantly with the zipper on his jacket.

"Yeah, well, maybe next time. I've had enough battering from last night." Zack exhaled, closing his eyes. He had no intention of reading anymore of that article. But heck! At least someone was giving him recognition, even if it was the wrong kind. His transition to CEO had been smoother than he'd thought possible. There was barely any publicity. He had his suspicions that it was because he started raving about becoming more renewable as soon as he obtained the post, hoping to introduce projects that made blocks of homes, similar to projects like BedZED he knew of down in London, that profited off using natural resources. It was possibly the worst thought not being associated towards managing the company. Heck, he could even remember on one of his first days being mistaken as one of the interviewees being directed to the basement as a postage and mail sorter than the

CEO. Not a good day for him, nor the receiving person on the other end.

"Man, I'm starving," Kyle declared as he rubbed his stomach and dropped his head back.

"I haven't eaten yet, so I can get Maria to cook us something. I'll call her in—"

"I do have feet, Zack," Kyle scoffed. "There's that major difference between us."

"What difference?" Zack asked, his brows furrowing together as he watched Kyle get up and head over to the large fridge, dead centre in the open-spaced kitchen.

Zack could hear the distant sound of rummaging until Kyle called out, "Found something." He returned with a packet of gammon slices, digging his fingers through them, hesitant before he was satisfied to shove a slice in his mouth.

"You're an idle bastard." Kyle chuckled, then dropped another slice of cut gammon into the dark, hungry abyss.

"*Idle?*"

Kyle nodded. "Don't fuck with yourself. You *know* you are."

"How so?" Zack scowled.

"*One.*" He lifted his forefinger up. "Take a look around. You didn't just get this from working your way up from the bottom. You got this because your family inherited a business that has lasted generations in your family," he stated, sitting on the arm of the chair. "*Two.* You never cook. I remember you telling me how you lived on Michelin-star restaurant cuisines and hired a personal chef at University because you didn't know how to cook. You probably don't even know what a fucking spatula is." Then he lifted his third finger up. "And you're just a lazy bastard overall." He smirked at the twist of surprise on Zack's face.

"I'm not *idle,*" Zack challenged.

"Er, yeah, you are," Kyle argued, shaking his head with disbelief.

"I run a business, which I don't see you doing. I'm not *idle.* I can do stuff. I think sex counts as one, *pal,*" Zack objected, narrowing his eyes at his friend, who was chuckling lightly to himself.

"You're so in denial, man. Heck, yeah, you own a business, but you practically only have to learn how to pick up a pen and sign your name and lecture here and there. Your employees do most of your work for you," Kyle declared. He burped as he dashed the packet onto the coffee table. "Just imagine you trying to live a normal life. No quick money, cars, not even any fucking *premium* gammon." He pointed to the empty packet he'd eaten seconds ago. "You wouldn't last." He smirked triumphantly. "I, on the other hand, would. I've been there, done that. Now, I have the luxury of putting my feet up because of the whollop of cash you put in my dad's hand."

"I bet I could," Zack blurted aggressively. "What could be so difficult?"

"Bet, you say?"

"That's what I said. I could do it with my eyes closed. Heck, I could do all the work my employees do and still end up on top," Zack proclaimed, thrusting his empty glass in the air. "I bet it's easy."

"Fine."

"Fine, what?" Zack said, ever so puzzled.

Kyle's lips drew further apart as the ends rose. "Let's make a bet then," he challenged.

***

UNKNOWN

A malodorous scent lingered as Eva ambled through the pitch-black alley. Ahead, the distinct silhouette of a figure continued on through the darkness, still unware of Eva, who was hidden in the shadows. The figure eventually came to a halt, racing to stand beneath the poorly lit orange street lamp. Hidden behind a filthy dumpster, she could see the faint creases across the figure's forehead and his troubled, hazel eyes. Holding her breath, she peered at the figure with suspicion as he turned to thump his fist on the battered, pastel green door. Steadily, she began to move up before taking residence at a second dumpster, where her view of the figure became much clearer. It was perhaps another ten seconds until the door opened inwards. She could barely hear a muffled voice, to which the suspect responded.

"Y-Yes. I-I have…it," the suspect stuttered, awkwardly fumbling with the inside pocket of his jacket.

This was her chance. If only the guys back at the station knew what she had been following up. The Chief would surely have to offer her that promotion once she caught a photo of the notorious gang leader's face. Holding her breath, she tried to concentrate on the muffled conversation, but unfortunately, whoever was standing opposite the suspect remained hushed. Eva held consciously onto her belt strap as she moved closer against the dumpster. From the corner of her eye, she could see what appeared to be a dispute between the two as the suspect shook his head, holding up his hands in surrender.

Without warning, the suspect turned to run before the tip of a suppressor peeked through the door and clicked. The man collapsed onto the floor, a pool of blood flooding the ground beside him. Eva jumped back, hitting a discarded glass bottle. Scrambling to her feet, she reached for her walkie-talkie, while the figure she hadn't seen earlier materialized, quickly approaching.

"This is Officer Jones. I have a murder on—"

She did not have a chance to finish her words as the tall figure snatched the radio from her hand and pushed her to the ground. The figure applied pressure on her neck with the gun, its metallic surface cold and firm against her skin.

"Fucking stay down, bitch!" he spat. "Call it off now before I fucking blow your brains out!"

Eva choked, gasping for air as she struggled to fight back. The figure placed the walkie-talkie towards her mouth and forcefully applied more pressure. "Now. Do it."

Struggling to defy the man, she nodded. As he began to ease the gun, Eva kicked the man in the groin. He moaned in agony, allowing her room to jump up. Eva picked up the walkie-talkie, bringing it towards her mouth when two solid arms suddenly took her hostage and snatched the device from her hands again. Eva screamed, kicking her feet out as her unknown captor pulled her along. The man she had kicked to the groin began to slowly get to his feet, groaning a little as he ordered, "Get her inside, quick. She's one of them. I'll remove this body. Let's just hope her little buddies didn't get the message."

"'Course," the stranger agreed. She remained restrained as he pulled her towards the door, her struggles useless. She was dragged into the dark building. Behind her, she could hear the door being shut, then the movement of the man reaching to the side.

"What we going to tell the boss?"

"We'll bring her along. I don't fancy cleaning up a cop," the man said, his voice gruff as he continued upfront.

"Won't they know if she's missing?" the figure who held her asked.

"We'll let the boss fix that. Now get her in the van."

Eva screamed, although it was barely audible as her mouth was covered with material, and suddenly everything went dark.

***

CLAIRE

RING. RING. RING.
Claire jumped suddenly out of her skin, throwing the plastic bowl full of sweet and salty popcorn into

the air, the kernels raining like edible paper confetti. Her heart rate hammered like crazy as she shoved off the blanket, muted the television, and sped in her own time—a *snail's pace*—to the kitchen to answer the phone.

"Hello?" she whispered, leaning her back gently onto the wooden kitchen counter.

"Claire, it's *me*. Why are you whispering?"

"Oh, Abbey! H—hey, heyyy." She coughed, awkwardly scratching the top of her head in embarrassment. *At least it wasn't a murderous killer,* she thought. "No reason."

"Okayyy. Well…I was just checking up. Seeing if things were going all right. I saw your advert on Facebook for the apartment. Any luck yet?" Abbey asked.

Claire groaned, running her right hand through her hair. "No. Nothing. Absolutely jackshit! It's ridiculous! I would have thought someone would have at least phoned up, but there's not been a single soul. Not that I blame anyone. It's because the stupid landlord has decided to put the rent up." She sighed, standing on her tip-toes. "Oh, Abbey, why did you leave me for that boyfriend of yours?" she teased.

"I'm actually asking myself that every day," Abbey joked.

"Don't lie, you love it."

"Well, have you tried the local universities? There has to be some students looking for a place to live, especially if all the nightlife, public transport, and food chains are nearby, and you live right damn in the centre of the city," Abbey suggested.

"Nope. Again. I don't think their finances stretch far enough with what my bloody landlord is asking," Claire grumbled.

She could hear shuffling from Abbey's line, a single pause before her friend piped up, "Oh, oh! Please tell me you're seeing someone, Claire?"

"No."

"Why not?"

"Abbey." Claire dragged her hand down her face with frustration. "I don't have time if I want to get that promotion," she explained, aware that wouldn't excuse her in Abbey's eyes.

"You've been waiting for that promotion for ages. That shouldn't stop you from dating," she lectured. "It's important that you don't end up like a cat lady, Claire."

Claire rolled her eyes. "That's such a cliché thing to say."

"Welcome to society. And, *Claire,* are you wearing that top with the '*I'm single and I don't want to mingle*' on it? You know, the one you always wear when you're having a lazy day in?" Abbey pointed out. Claire could imagine the peak of her eyebrow rocketing up alongside that.

"*So?* I like that top."

"Yeah, and you're twenty-four. Anyway, I gotta go. Matthew is burning the food; I can smell it. I'm sure you've smashed your promotion. You always have your shit together. I'll text you later or something," she said, ending the call.

Claire sighed, then mimicked Abbey as she turned her hand into a sock puppet, "*You need to date. Blah. Blah.*" She paused, dropping her hand, then glancing to her top. "I like this top."

***

ZACK

"Okay, what? A bet?" Zack reiterated, scratching the tip of his nose.

"Yeah, you've given me an idea," Kyle agreed, slapping his knees as he got to his feet. "We'll make a bet. Besides, every CEO pretty much goes on a break. The business can just run itself and you could have flown off to Las Vegas for all they know." He slowly grinned from ear to ear.

"I'm confused, man. What are you getting at?" Zack got to his own feet, watching as Kyle wandered around the room, biting the tip of his thumb and going back and forth between the fireplace and Zack.

Kyle suddenly exclaimed, "I got it!" Picking up a magazine from off the side, he jerked it in front of Zack's face, jabbing at a single word. "This," he cried out. "Undercover. You. You do this! You'll do as you said. Pose as an employee in your firm and learn that I was right all along. You won't be able to cope," he said, triumphantly crossing his arms as Zack snatched the magazine out of his hands.

"So what? Is this how I'm supposed to prove I can *be normal?*" Zack muttered, confused.

"Yes. And think about it. It's like an unofficial inspection of your own company if you want to see it like that, too. I know you're competitive, Zack, so

I know you'll accept." Kyle smiled, adjusting his fedora slightly.

"I'm just—wait, so, to prove I'm not idle…wait—hang on." Zack itched some of the stubble cloaking his chin. "So, you want me to put myself on hold, go into my business, pretend to be an employee for however long just to prove I'm not idle as you say I am?" he explained, watching as Kyle's face lit up.

"Yep."

"Do you even know how silly you sound? I mean…" Zack snickered, waving his hands gently about by his sides. "You want me to—you have got to be joking!" He shook his head in disbelief as he pulled out his iPhone. "Ah, great." Zack threw his phone back onto the side. "Dad ain't so happy about my appearance last night. Another fucking thing he'll have me for. I swear, what is even the point of me running it?"

"*I'll make it'll worth your time*," Kyle sang, ignoring what he previously said.

"Name your price," Zack sternly said, his lips curving. "I might as well. It's not like I'm really doing anything."

"I get choice of any of your cars. And you have to go on a date with my cousin if you fail," Kyle demanded. "And I don't mean Jenna. I mean my cousin, Trevor."

"Really?"

"Yes. It's just a bit of fun, Zacky-boy. Or are you too chicken to go through with it?" Kyle teased.

"No, I'll do it." Zack held out his hand.

"Don't you want your side of the bargain?"

"Nope. I just like the good ol' spirit of competition," he replied.

"Well, okay," Kyle said, then shook Zack's hand. "Oh, and by the way. I didn't say how long this bet will last. So thanks for signing this deal with the devil." He smirked, gripping Zack's hand.

If there was one thing about Zack, he didn't like losing.

CHAPTER TWO

CLAIRE

Claire had never felt so exhausted. If she hadn't been well aware that her alarm clock was the life vessel towards her living, eating, and surviving in this world, she would have smashed it, chopped it, and burned it to pieces. *She hated mornings.* She was pretty sure her mirror hated her mornings too; her hair was a bird's nest, dribble was still snaking out of her mouth, and—she might as well have called them teabags—she had small bags under her eyes. Thank God she didn't have anyone in her bed, because even her toothpaste seemed repulsed to want to touch her stinky breath—a gift by yours truly, the retainers.

She sluggishly headed out of the bedroom, took five minutes in the bathroom, then forced herself into the kitchen. *She could always detour back to bed,* she thought. No, she forced herself to make a coffee. Its power to knock some energy into her was evident as she felt its fierce embrace slide down the back of her throat. Ah, coffee, her *only* companion in the mornings. It didn't bug, didn't moan or speak; it knew the only way to survive the mornings was to hush up and let a person relax. If this happened to be a set scene for a TV advertisement, she'd nailed it. Cut the crap out of being ebullient at the crack of dawn, look half-asleep, and move like a sloth, then you've nailed it. This should be how coffee should be served.

Seven-thirty was already moving on; Claire had just only happened to slip on her second black ankle boot. Sitting on the edge of the sofa, she groaned as she slumped forward, begging herself to go back to sleep. But it made no difference. She got up, shoved on her blue parka jacket with the white fluff around the hood, locked up the apartment, and headed for the bus stop.

The bus was not tardy this morning. It arrived dead on time, exactly what was predicted on the timetable downloaded to her phone. *Thank God,* she thought. There were plenty of vacant seats. And there were the familiar faces of commuters she saw pretty much every day. Some looked shattered, just like Claire felt. The journey was the same—long queues of traffic, so many frequent stops—and there was always someone who decided to fall asleep, someone who just happened to slump awkwardly onto Claire's shoulder. But, *alas!* She made it, getting off at her stop to follow the marching congregation of crowds meandering through the business district. Claire felt lucky that her workplace, the towering rectangle compared to its neighbours, was not far from her bus stop.

Bensons Corporations. The location of its headquarters. Some old man, or whoever the CEO was, sat right at the top of the floor while all his working ants, like Claire, shared the floors below. She entered the building, swiping her ID card to get through the barriers, smiling as she caught sight of her other close friend, Darren, snooping through the collection of visitors' magazines.

"Morning, sunshine." He smiled, the cheekiness prevalent in his small dimples on either side of his cheeks.

"Oh, why must you remind me?" Claire said, playfully frowning as they headed side by side towards the elevated space holding five lifts on either side.

They stepped in one lift. "Excited? Nervous?" Darren said, nudging her in the shoulder.

"I'm…anxious," she replied. "I just want to get it over with. I need this promotion. It will help pay the bills."

"Oh, yeah, you know, I saw some guy looking at your advert pinned on the board this morning. Maybe they'll be interested. And you know you have nothing to worry about," he encouraged as they stepped out onto the sixth floor. They passed through the lines of desks holding her fellow colleagues captive, making their way to the department's kitchen to quickly snag a cup of tea.

"Yeah, maybe," Claire muttered, flopping into the chair.

"Here, cheer up. You need to be more positive. I bet you'll get a phone call sooner than you think. And, girl, you know, we'll be celebrating in no time when you get that promotion, eh?" He winked, filling two empty cups with hot water.

"Morning!" another voice blurted.

Claire and Darren looked over. Jason, one of their friendly colleagues, entered the room, taking his empty mug to the sink.

"Hey!" Darren cheerfully replied.

Jason was one of those men Claire was slightly confused about. Not that she was confused about him as a person, but she couldn't tell if she had a bit of a crush on him or she just liked his character. The man did have a nice ass, though.

"How was your weekend?" Jason asked, drying his hands on a tea-towel.

"Good. Just the usual. Parties, just like back when I was that daring, young, gay teenager," Darren teased, waving his hand with sass.

"And you?"

Claire blinked. "Ah, doing some catch-up work, but I did watch a movie."

"Good, good. Well, hey, good luck today, Claire. I'm cheering for you," he said, whooping his right fist in the air briefly. "See you guys around, then." He exited the kitchen.

"He fancies the socks off you," Darren declared, raising his right brow.

"Er, no, he doesn't," she disagreed. "What makes you even think that, I'll never know."

"I just know."

Their conversation ceased as Monica, the red-haired devil, as gorgeous as a top model, broke into the kitchen. "Chop, chop, you two. We're having a staff meeting," she stated, possibly spitting fire at the end of her tongue.

"Thanks, *Monica*," he sneered. "I would love to just throw those black Gucci heels she wears into her face." He rolled his sleeves up.

"A'ight, a'ight, easy, tiger. Let's just get in there." Claire chuckled, guiding Darren like a mother would do to a child, out of the kitchen and into the office space.

The majority of staff were huddled around, some quickly sneaking past, to not get caught being late. Darren and Claire pushed on towards the back, watching as Clive Graves, department manager, exited his exclusive office holding a pile of paper under his arm. He was a grey-haired man, broad, and he was very boastful about those huge bullet-sized arms. Susan—the office gossiper—had accused him of using steroids. She'd also thrown in that, apparently, he was sleeping around with Monica.

"Okay, settle down," Graves ordered, loosening his tie a little. "I know that some of you have been very anxious as to who will become co-department manager for some months now. But, alas…" He sighed, leaning his hefty hands onto a desk. "I've decided…"

Claire's heart was thumping like a drum. The tension was unbelievable. She wanted it so badly.

Darren squeezed her arm reassuringly. "You've got this," he whispered.

Graves opened his mouth. "That person is," he said, driving Claire even crazier by the second, "Ms. Monica Andrews." He clapped his hands along with the rest of the office except Darren and

Claire. She slumped into her chair, defeated.

"How is this even possible?" she muttered, dropping her head into her hands.

"Claire. I'm so sorry—"

"I worked so, so damn hard," she interrupted, passionately erasing the physical sight of Monica being congratulated at the front until only a few gathered around her. "I had employee of the year last year. I worked overtime. I even helped Marketing improve targets for customer relationships. It just doesn't make sense, Darren." She wanted to cry.

"I know, babe. I know you did," Darren said, sitting on the adjacent desktop chair and clasping her hands. "This isn't because of you. This is because she's manipulated him with sex."

"And how's that fair? It's bad enough women still get shit in the workplace. Eurgh!" she complained, slapping her hand across her forehead. "I'm sorry if I sound like a bitch. It just sucks. I genuinely would have been happier if it were anyone else. Just not her. She makes me so mad."

"Er, don't apologise, babes. I feel the hatred just as you do. Graves is being so unfair," he agreed.

"Now what? It's not like I could go and complain. And now I still can't fix my rent problem," she sighed.

"And I told you, if it gets to that, you can move in with me, babes," Darren said.

"That's why I love you." Claire smiled tightly.

***

ZACK

Zack leaned back in his leather desktop chair, drumming his fingers together as if he were praying—although, if he could, he would pray that his father would stop pestering him. It didn't help he had gotten lectured on the phone last night on how important it was for him to maintain his father's positive relationships within the elite circles. How his father found out was another thing. Maybe his old man had connections with the MI5.

"So, you were joking about all that yesterday, right?" Zack suggested, watching as Kyle, this time in bright green chinos, sat on the single black leather armchair opposite Zack's desk.

"Er, no. You're going through with it. And thanks to me, I've made it ten times more possibly real," he replied, eagerly unwrapping the sweet wrapper from the mint he'd picked up from the bowl on the side table next to him. It was supposed to be for visitors.

"Ah, well," Zack sighed, flipping over folders on his desk to illustrate his point. "It's not *like* I have *much* to do," he said sarcastically.

"Deal's been made. And it's a bit of fun." Kyle crunched on the mint. "Anyway, I saw this advert on floor six. And might I just add, your building is still a fucking maze. Anyway..." He swallowed. "Someone is advertising for a flatmate. Down in the city centre, so not far from here. So there's your accommodation sorted for some months to come." Kyle smirked proudly, leaning his leg over the other.

"Oh, okay," Zack sneered, "I'm *supposed* to move in with someone. I thought it was just me working undercover here and *learning* to be normal?"

"*Exactly*. How else are you gonna get the full experience? I even say you budget yourself." He clicked the roof of his mouth. "Say, eight hundred pounds a month or something," Kyle suggested.

"What? You have got to be kidding. How am I supposed to eat out? What about my weekly massage sessions? Or the gym! I'd blow it all in less than a week!" Zack exclaimed, frowning at Kyle, who was looking greener with greed than his own pair of chinos.

"And there's your true colours, you snob." Kyle grinned.

"I genuinely despise you," Zack remarked.

"Ah, isn't our friendship beautiful?"

"No."

Kyle chuckled. "Let us not be negative, shall we? All I'm asking you to do is live with this person. You can toy around with the business, Zacky-boy. So, cheer up," Kyle encouraged, getting up to his feet. "I had the audacity of neatly placing the advert in your blazer pocket. Aren't I lovely? And guess what? You're so unrecognisable in your own position that you don't even need a disguise! Farewell." Mockingly waving at Zack, he headed out the two tall doors.

Zack crumpled up a piece of paper and threw it at the door.

As much as Zack wanted to throw Kyle into space, he was a man of his word. That evening he telephoned the addressee, partly expecting to hear a male...instead, delightfully, he melted with eagerness at hearing a woman on the other end.

"Hello? Who is this?" she asked, her appealing, fairly soft tone spurring Zack's appetite despite the meal Maria had placed before him that was cooked by a private chef.

He leaned his elbows on the counter, thumbing on how he should respond. He had to be quick because he could hear her hesitation, from the distance her voice seemed to travel as she huffed in frustration. "It's...Zack C—Zack Chase. I'm enquiring on the rent," he piped up, stroking his stubbly chin.

"Oh, sorry." She anxiously chuckled. "Erm, I just wasn't expecting even a word of interest. I th—er, sorry. The rent, yeah. Bad day, so I'm kinda—sorry, I shouldn't be—"

Zack's smile broadened deviously. "Not at all. I wouldn't blame you for being so suddenly anxious from the delivery of such a handsome tone," he teased.

He'd expected her to at least quiver or stutter on the spot, like he was used to. She did not. She took him by surprise with her witty remark. "Oh, okay, *buddy*. Yeah, *sure*. Look, the rent has gone up. So it's four hundred seventy-five pounds at the moment. Take it or leave it, Mr. Casanova," she said, putting *him* on the spot.

Zack swallowed. Not usually what he was used to. But he liked it, strangely enough.

"A'ight," he agreed. "Where do I sign my name?"

"Yeah, *okay*, sure—*wait*, really?" she buzzed.

"Sure," he replied, tapping his finger on the counter. "This *Mr. Casanova* is interested." He licked his bottom lip.

"Erm, yeah. Well, when do you think you can—"

"Now," he interrupted. "I'll meet you as soon as possible, and we'll have this ship sailing in no time." He sat up, excited for some reason when he heard a short squeal of her own excitement.

"Okay, that's cool. How about tomorrow? I'll forward you the address to this number," she said. It was apparent to him that she felt awkward because she cleared her throat several times.

"Beautiful. Until then," he uttered, instantly deciding he was going to like parts of this situation.

"Sure, see you tomorrow," she responded. *You hear that fellas?*

CHAPTER THREE

CLAIRE

She'd read a book last night. She'd also cried. *A lot.* But then she cheered up a little when that stranger called up. He sounded cocky. Not like how the protagonist's lover in this book sounded, *no*, that male character was a raw gentleman. Not only was the plot cliché, springing up the stereotypes of masculinity and femininity, it was also awfully addictive. Claire could not deny her toes curled at the obnoxiously attractive male whose mane of long, tousled hair shimmered down onto his bronzed chest while, of course, the damsel in distress fainted into his strong arms. And how the sex was mind-blowingly so perfect the protagonist cried. Yeah, it was shit. *Read a horror next time*, she'd told herself.

Going in to work was a troubling task at best. She did not want to go in.

"I still can't believe yesterday," Claire sighed, stirring the sugar around in her tea.

"Me neither. You should see how she keeps fucking prancing around the office. It's as if she thinks she's bloody won the presidential election. Claire, I know you wanted the promotion, but I'm just glad you're not sharing it with creepy old Graves," Darren confessed, putting the bottle of milk back into the fridge.

"Ah, I suppose," she replied, clinking the spoon around the diameter of the cup.

At that moment, Jason entered, his hands in his trouser pockets and the pocket watch he liked attached to his waist jacket, swinging like a pendulum against his chest. His brows lifted up as if to say hello before they dropped as he stopped a footstep away from Claire.

"Hey, can we talk?" he asked, itching his forehead.

"Sure." Claire shrugged her shoulders.

"Erm," Jason began, uncomfortably glancing over to Darren, who was curiously watching this all play out until he took the memo and dashed out the kitchen.

Claire quizzically looked behind her, wondering why he left.

Jason anxiously laughed. "Erm. I was wondering if you wanted to go out over the weekend?"

"Er, like where?"

"The movies or...well, the movies," he said, a flare of redness inflaming his cheeks.

Claire shrugged her shoulders once again. "Sure, why not? Just text me the details."

"Great, great." Jason smiled, nodding as he said his farewell, then left the kitchen on his way back into the ant farm, *the office.*

Darren whooped quietly as he swooped back in, smacking his knee as he hopped. "I knew it!" he exclaimed. "I told you! I told you!"

Claire frowned. "Told me what?"

"He likes you!"

"No, no. Wait. This isn't a date," she disagreed, shaking her head.

"It is, babes." Darren smirked. "You just entered first class on the love boat." He winked, lifting and dropping his eyebrows.

"No, no, no." She shook her head.

"Yes—oh," he teased, "he's gonna relieve some of that tension I know has been building up in you for a while, oh, oh, yes, yes."

"I'm not sexually frustrated!"

Darren chuckled, ignoring her completely as they headed into the office and took their desks.

Claire rolled her eyes at Darren's immaturity as he pretended to shoot an arrow over to Jason, who was sitting towards the front of the department, typing madly away. There was just no way this was a date.

She turned on her computer, opening various spreadsheets. For the next several hours, she would relentlessly work non-stop until she could no longer feel her toes or fingers.

***

"Urgh," she grumbled, stretching her arms. She'd managed to finish the spreadsheet covering last month's financial outlook, editing and updating

31

comments to suggest where there could be improvement for their product.

"I'm beat." Darren yawned, glancing at his wrist watch. "It's five. Time to go."

Claire agreed, switching the desktop off. She was busy collecting her pencil case and water bottle when the beep of her phone alerted her. Expecting a message of either a relative or friend, she cursed aloud when she read the single line. "Shit, shit," she repeated, throwing her phone quickly in her bag.

"What's up?" he asked, putting on his bright yellow jacket.

"I forgot that I was supposed to be meeting someone later," she replied, getting to her feet and putting on her parka jacket. "He's coming to check out the apartment."

"*He?*"

"Yes."

"And you forgot to tell me that someone was interested *because?*" Darren crossed his arms, scrutinizing her with his blue eyes.

"Yeah, sorry. I forgot myself," she admitted, placing the strap of her handbag across her shoulder.

"*Erh, huh.* Well, what does he sound like?"

Claire snorted, shaking her head as they both headed towards the lift shaft. "Like a *cocky* bastard."

Darren lifted his eyebrows, pressing the call button. "*Really?*"

"Yeah." She nodded. "Just…I only care if he can pay the rent. That's all I'm asking for," she insisted, combing her hair with her fingers towards her right shoulder.

"Hmm, *cocky*. I wonder," Darren said, grinning from ear to ear. "If he's gay, I'd love to mingle with him. Although, did I tell you about that next-door neighbour I have down the corridor?"

"No, why?" Claire swiped her ID card as they passed through reception.

"Sweet mother, he's *handsome*." Darren dazed off into the distance.

Claire chuckled, stopping as her phone buzzed again. "Okay, now either I've agreed to allow a spy to move into my apartment or he's just a good stalker. Apparently, he's outside," she said, gaping a little as she refused to believe that he meant directly *here*, right now.

"Like outside, as in *outside?*"

"Yeah." She nodded. "I think I should actually run. He might be some seriously messed-up dude," she joked.

They stopped outside adjacent to the large, faintly orange pots filled with plants standing outside on either end of the revolving doors. Darren sat on the edge of the stone wall that led down to the bottom of the road, tucking his finger into his loafers where he had an uncomfortable itch.

"So, what now?" he piped up. "We waiting for him? How do you even know what he looks like?"

Claire shrugged her shoulders. "*Exactly*. I don't know. He said he was around here. I'll text him now." She got her phone again, hovering her fingers across the screen, stopping at the urgency of Darren's shrill tone.

"Oi, oi, check him out over there," he said,

pointing his finger rudely at a man who was leaning his foot against the wall, his head down as he looked at his phone. "Handsome devil."

Claire glanced, strangely enough agreeing. He had a *killer* jawline, stretching in a V-shape near enough, tousled raven hair, and broad shoulders that went on for days. Questions flew around in her mind. *Did he work here? Did he have a girlfriend? Was he related to Greek gods?* Cliché, she knew. But it had made her subconsciously bite down on her tongue. Wasn't that the case with every attractive person, though? Even if they weren't asking for it, she was gonna give him the attention.

"Okay, he's fit," she declared, lifting her eyebrows as the stretch of his blue t-shirt followed the contour of his figure.

"Think he's single?"

"Dunno. Just, I feel strangely inferior. I shouldn't even be looking at him," she said, squeezing her fingers into her palms. "I really badly want to keep staring at him, though." She paused, her phone beeped, begging her to detach her gaze away from the beautiful specimen. "Apparently, he's—" Her face began to turn white. "He's—"

"He's what?" Darren demanded.

Claire swallowed. "He's sitting on a wall."

Darren's smile beamed. "You think it's him?" He jerked his head to the right, directly towards the stranger they'd both greedily undressed with their eyes.

"I hope not," she confessed. Then she quickly looked down to her phone, typed a message, and waited anxiously for the reply.

Seconds later, she got the message, and that man sitting on the wall stood up.

Holy mercy of cheese, she thought.

***

Zack felt repulsed as he adjusted the collar of the blue and black squared flannel he was wearing open over the top of his blue t-shirt. He *missed* his own clothes. It felt cheap, nasty, and uncomfortable against his skin. Apparently, though, this was the height of fashion, as Kyle had kindly put it—back in *his* teenage years.

His eyes searched the crowd, wondering if he should turn back. This sounded stupid. Why was he doing this again? He felt silly walking up to his own building pretending to be another, and it offended him that not a single face recognised him. Was his own face so much of a disguise?

Ahead, he caught sight of a woman hesitantly walking straight into his path. Her fairly dark brown hair was swooped over her right shoulder, her lips perky and pink, and her eyes, a natural brown, seemingly glimmered and it struck him by surprise. She wasn't massively attractive like models he'd fooled about with, no, she had *something* else. He couldn't explain it, but it fascinated him. Her head was oval-shaped, she had a beauty mark below her left eye, and there were a few natural blemishes.

Their paths collided. She stopped one step from him, and he did the same. She held her breath; whirl washed in the depths of his eyes.

"Are you Zack Chase?" she asked eventually,

35

startling him by surprise at the sound of his name—minus the surname—coming from her lips.

He stiffened his posture, slowly grinning. "Yes," he said, deliberately licking his bottom lip. "You must be Claire?"

"Yes, er, can you give me one second?" she asked.

"Sure."

Then not nearly as slow as she moved towards him, she quickly swept away to whoever was waiting for her near the entrance of the building.

***

CLAIRE

Claire tugged on Darren's shoulder, hissing, "What am I supposed to do? It's him, a'ight! I can't have him in my apartment. I'd be too scared to take a shit!"

"Whoa, whoa, chill," Darren consoled, grabbing both side of her arms. "Snap out of it. Fucking hell!"

"But look at him, Darren," she whispered. She quickly looked behind her; he was leaning up against the wall again.

"Stop being such a drama queen. I'm jealous, babes. You've got potentially a sex god in your apartment. Don't take that for granted," he lectured, squeezing her arm. "Now stop being a pussy." He pecked her left cheek and then slapped her back to spur her on.

Claire's legs really didn't know how to function

then. She had trouble moving them, as if she'd forgotten suddenly how to walk. Taking a deep breath, she headed towards him.

"Sorry," she began, pausing as his beautiful eyes looked up to her. "My friend needed directions. I presume you want to see the apartment now?"

He nodded. "After you," he said chivalrously, placing his hand out towards the road.

"Erm, cool." She nodded. "Just so you know, I don't have a car, so we're gonna have to catch the bus," she explained, feeling hot and sweaty.

***

ZACK

Zack cringed inside. "Of course, that's fine," he lied through his teeth.

"Erm," she said as they stood at the stop, waiting for her bus to come. "How did you know I worked here?"

Zack froze on the spot. "Some friend I know who works here found your advert at the workplace," he lied once again…well, partly anyway.

"Oh. Cool then."

"I'm surprised," he said, startling Claire.

"About what?"

"Well, aren't I Mr. Casanova? I was expecting a witty remark," he teased with a grin.

"Ha ha. No, I—well—yeah. Oh, look! Here's the bus!" she exclaimed.

Zack had never ridden a bus. It was definitely an

experience. Jam packed. He couldn't even confer with Claire, who managed to snag a seat, leaving him standing up at the front, holding onto a strap that he at first presumed was for decoration. He'd nearly learned the hard way, though. Some old woman even decided to ram her trolley into his leg, obviously forgetting there was a living soul there.

"Are they always like that?" he asked, frowning as he rubbed his shoulder. They had got off at a stop that was just outside the block of the two-floored apartments Claire resided in. He was thankful to see the bus go. *Never again*, he shuddered.

Claire snorted. "Why? Not your cup of tea usually?"

Zack cocked his left eyebrow as they headed into the building. "Oh? No, it was *charmingly* splendid," he said sarcastically as they took the flight of curved stairs.

"Ha, yeah, you looked as if you've never even been on one. Not for you, is it, *pretty boy?*" she joked as she dug her hands into her bag for a set of keys to open up her apartment.

"*Pretty boy,* eh? I thought you were in dire need of a flatmate? Aren't you supposed to be impressing me? Not offending me?" he teased, watching as her cheeks tinged a little red. She was becoming a bit of challenge, which he was beginning to like.

"I did not, nor do I need one," she lied, pushing her key into the lock. "I was just *doing* a civilian service by *offering* my home up."

***

CLAIRE

Her home was on show. She just hoped she had remembered to put away her washing. It was already awkward enough with this fella without adding a pair of knickers lying on the sofa or on top of some basket.

"Okay," she exhaled, stepping to the side to allow him to enter through. "This is what's on offer," she said.

"Do you also come with that offer?" he remarked, his cheeky grin spreading quicker than a house on fire.

"Oh, very funny," she muttered, rolling her eyes.

***

ZACK

So, she was *different,* Zack thought. He had to step his game up.

She introduced him to the kitchen, pointed to the appliances, explained that the oven could sometimes be dodgy, and they should form a rota on who does the washing up. Then came the bedrooms, two separate on either side of the corridor, and the bathroom at the end of it.

"Looks...cosy," he observed. This was all entirely too small. *How on earth do people even live like this?* he thought. Even the bathtub appeared like only an arm could fit.

"Well, it ain't no Ritz, but it does the job," she replied.

"I'll take it," he confidently said.

"Wait, *really?"*

Zack nodded, crossing his arms.

***

CLAIRE

His sleeves tugged up, and so did Claire's interest: veiny, hairy bold arms, a woman's weakness. She wondered how much he lifted. *No,* she scolded herself.

"Okay, c—cool," she agreed. "I just need you to sign this agreement I briefly—"

"Yes," he interrupted. "Pass it over."

Claire left to retrieve it, placed it in front of him. "Here you go," she said, offering him a pen.

"Thanks, darling."

"I ain't your *darling,* Mister," she said, crossing her arms. "When are you thinking of moving in?"

"Tonight," he replied, without looking up.

"Oh."

"Yeah, so, cheer up." He smiled as he got to his feet. "I'll be seeing you very soon."

Chapter Four

ZACK

Zack had the exact same unpleasant taste lounging in the back of his throat as he got onto the third bus of the day...so far. He hated the sight of it. On the tawdry, moss green seats sat other passengers, unbothered by the filthy environment. He couldn't understand why it didn't trouble them. Was this normal? Were dry stains, sticky chewing gum, and packets of rubbish stuffed down the sides of seats or carelessly shuffled around the floor *normal?* Had humanity gone insane? Was it worth all this hassle just to prove a point? He didn't know. Nor did he want to know how the middle-aged, greasy grey-haired woman sitting at the front holding her trolley close to her was biting on the ends of her nails as if they were a feast. Zack pulled a face of grimace. *What next? Appetite for flesh?* he thought.

His phone began to buzz, as did his ears when some lad pushing to the back played his music obnoxiously loud from the mini speakers on his phone whilst adjusting his snapback.

"Hello?" he answered, shuffling closer to the window, but not too close, afraid he'd come into contact with that sticky piece of pink chewing gum he'd noticed earlier.

"Mr. Benson, it's Olivia," a nasally voice replied.

"Ah, Olivia," Zack reiterated, hoping that even his personal assistant wouldn't be able to sniff out from his background noise that he was on a bus. He wanted to hold onto some dignity.

"I'm sorry to pester you, sir, but I'm just letting you know that the council has accepted your plans for construction on their site. The agreed cost is set at six hundred and fifty thousand pounds. Would you like me to follow up with an email?" she asked. He could imagine her pushing the rims of her glasses up, a habit he'd gotten used to seeing.

"Yes, that's fine. Could you also make sure to send out that email I have saved on my laptop? Send it to all department managers. I want them to be aware of the next project coming up in this area," he said, trying to refrain himself from being distracted at the sight of another passenger two seats down and vertically opposite him snacking on a greasy, dripping meat sandwich. It made him want to gag.

"Certainly, Mr. Benson," she replied.

"Oh, and keep me posted regularly. I'm going to be away from my desk," he instructed her before ending the phone call and slipping the device into his flannel's breast pocket.

Was it humanly possible to run a business that required him to answer emails, phone calls, show up at events, hear from the other two branches the business also ran, and play a hoax as an employee? Well, maybe if you weren't Elijah Benson, his father. But for Zack, Kyle was right—there was at most very little for him to do. No one knew his face. That was why changing the company's path to go green was his toolkit to making a name for himself rather than relying on his father's successful past as UK's leading house-building company. It was a lot to live up to. He wanted to scrap cheap fossil-fuelled homes and construct greener, affordable housing. It was something he knew he couldn't even breathe down his father's neck unless he wanted an early death sentence.

Alas. No one could understand how much it meant to see his penthouse creeping into view after it felt like an eternity trekking up that hill. He was actually quite proud of himself. For a person who didn't ever use public transport, he'd worked out, with the help of Google Maps, how to find the nearest bus stop to his home. It didn't mean he enjoyed it, nor did he relish the fact that he'd managed—no, instead he had wished he had Wickes, his personal driver, chauffeuring him back and forth.

"A'ight, Zacky boy." Kyle smiled, lunging over to him. Not in bright-coloured chinos, but basketball-type shorts just stopping inches away from his hairy knees. His friend, *strangely* enough, was in his penthouse.

"Again? What do you call this?" he said, walking

into the central room and immediately blinking several times. "What's been going on in here?" he exclaimed, planting his hands out to the side, hinting at the presence of his brother, Jared, relaxing on the couch with two barely clothed women lying against his naked chest. "I'm sorry, since when did my home become an open house?"

"Oh, hey, bro." Jared's tone was gruff as he lazily smiled. "Hope you don't mind, I was visiting, and Kyle here was just in the middle of a small get-together. I think your name got lost in the invite. I hope you don't mind." He coughed as he stretched his arms to embrace the women closer.

Jared was four years younger, barely an adult in Zack's eyes. Their features were similar, only his brother had brownish hair, and he was a lot shorter than Zack.

"Ha! No, it's fine! So, while you're at it, why don't you go fuck in my bedsheets too?" Zack hissed, dropping his hands onto his hips.

"Whoa, whoa! Angry man who's gonna shit his boxers, calm!" Kyle interjected, hushing his finger over his lips at the sleeping pair either side of Jared.

"What the fuck do you call this, Kyle? Just because I'm—wait, have you told him about it?" he muttered, jabbing his finger at Jared.

"Yeah, of course."

"Ah, great," he sighed, shaking his head.

"No, it's cool," Kyle insisted. "Look, I'll drop you off if that stops you from making a scene."

"Fuck off, Kyle." He sighed. "And I'd rather get the bus...in fact, I will. I'm not losing this bet. I know what you're trying to do! So fuck it. Excuse me. I've got to pack," he spat, pushing him aside.

"Whatever you say," Kyle said before calling out after him, "you might want to be careful of your bathroom sink. One of the girls, Becky, was sick in it earlier!"

***

ZACK

And here Zack was again, squashed up against a window by a scruffy-looking guy who'd taken the seat next to him. *It just had to be Zack, didn't it?* He held his duffel bag protectively on his lap, his black hoodie up, a frown on his face, and every stop they'd passed, he begged it was this man's stop. He hated buses. *Hated them.*

And now it was raining. *Great.*

Heaving his wet duffel bag and tugging on his mini suitcase, he stopped outside door number forty, feeling the slick slap of water *still* cascading down his forehead. He knocked on the door, tugging off his hood at the same time.

The door opened inwards.

"Well, you look like a *wet rat*," she remarked, her arms crossed over her pink camisole top.

"Oh, ha ha," he replied, his voice tight and hoarse from the wet, chilly cold. "Can I come in or do I have to wait here like I had to wait for that bus?" he grumbled.

"You do travel light," she commented as he heaved his suitcase into the corridor. "Are you sure you're planning to stay? Did you even have furniture where you came from?" She followed him as he slapped his duffel bag onto the side of the sofa and then ran his fingers through his wet black locks over again and again.

"Shower?" he asked as he rubbed the palms of his hands together.

"Same place as before. Down the end of the corridor by the bedrooms," she replied, staring.

"Take a picture, it'll last longer." He smirked.

"Pssf," she hissed, rolling her eyes. "Trust me, I wouldn't really care to," she lied.

"Whatever makes you sleep at night," he replied, picking up his duffel bag from off the side and whistling then as he headed towards the bathroom.

***

CLAIRE

Claire frowned. *Jackass,* she thought. Remind her why she agreed to do this again? Oh, yeah, the rent. And probably because of his *abs. No.* Definitely not.

In the kitchen, she was adding the spaghetti pasta into the hot, boiling water when she heard him next. She definitely, absolutely, most certainly did not drop the rest of the packet when mean ol' abs walked in.

"Shit," she cursed, bending down to pick up the mess.

Oh, minus one for her. Bonus points for his apparently egotistical self. She did drop them, not because he startled her, because she heard him coming, but because Mr. Abs made a grand entrance. *Literally.* Oh, she would have paid her neighbours to have seen the mean pecs on him, the parallel train tracks chiselled to his chest, and that dangerous upside-down triangle leading into treachery. *Oh, mother of pancakes.* This was not good.

"Can—" she cleared her throat, "can I help you?" Blinking, she looked anywhere but his chest.

"The hot water. It's different than the shower I had. Do you mind?" he said, faintly grinning. It was deliberate. She knew he had her trapped, *for the time being,* where he wanted her. Did she also mention he was wearing nothing but a white towel riding low on his hips? No?

"I suppose," she squeaked, turning down the gas on the hob before following him to the bathroom.

He stepped aside as she headed in, switched on the shower, and turned the dial slowly to the left. "Here," she said, "you just have to turn it this way. It should have already been on hot, but I guess I forgot to change it when I had a cold shower," she explained, slowly pulling her arm back from behind the shower curtain.

"Oh, I see."

"Cool."

His hand went for his towel, immediately ringing alarm bells. "Whoa, whoa!" she exclaimed, covering her eyes. "I'm *still* here, y'know?"

"I know."

She pulled her hands away, raising her eyebrows. His towel was still intact. "Keep it hidden, pal," she warned. "There's two people under this roof, you know."

Zack was biting back so hard. "Won't happen, again, *Ma'am,*" he apologised, smiling as she daggered her eyes at him.

She left then, hot-headed and disappointed at her female hormones. If there was one thing she wanted to be good at, it was singling out the jerks. She had barely become acquainted with the man and already he was gonna give her the full Monty show.

***

CLAIRE

How does one eat? How does one chew? How does one swallow?

She probably didn't seem conscious of how she was eating. Picturing herself as she sat there, swirling her fork into the spaghetti and slowly chewing the odd meatball without making a mess made it, somewhat indescribably, a joke. This was *Claire.* And if she knew herself, like the torture she'd put her parents through anytime they'd took the night off cooking, she knew she was a messy eater.

It was *his* fault. Yes, *he* sat opposite her, digging into the bowl of spaghetti she'd kindly offered to share. Now she regretted it. *Big time.* She wanted to shovel it down her throat, but that annoying nag inside ordered her different. How it made sense, she didn't know. *Because just look at* him, her nag told her. *He's God's gift sent from heaven.*

"This is nice." He dug his fork aggressively into

the bowl as he wolfed down his fifth round of spaghetti. "Oh God, you don't even realise how hungry I am," he moaned, rubbing his right hand across his chest, satisfied.

Claire blinked several times.

"I mean *this*..." Zack grinned slowly, pausing his fork somewhere in the middle of the bowl. "This is fucking tasty. Like, I didn't even think it would taste this good," he confessed, shaking his head with a smile as he dived for another bite.

"Gee, thanks," she mumbled. "I don't know whether to take that as a compliment or what." Her eyes were torn at the sight of spaghetti sauce speckled on his white v-cut shirt.

"So," he began, completely changing the topic. "What's there to know about Ms. Claire Winter? Huh? I think now's a good time to get into the nitty gritty." His eyes briefly met hers before lashing hungrily back to the bowl of food.

She shrugged her shoulders.

"Oh, c'mon. You can't tell me you seriously have nothing to tell," he replied, disappointed.

"Well, maybe I don't," she meekly suggested, digging her fork pointlessly into a meatball she knew she wasn't going to eat. "Anyway, I think it's me who should be doing the asking."

"Oh, yeah?"

"Yeah. I mean, I don't know anything about you. And you know nothing about me. For all you know, I could be the classic femme fatale, luring male victims into my trap before dishing their heads on a silver platter. And let's be real, you were quick on moving in," she said openly, jabbing her fork into the meatball again.

"Wow, was not expecting that." He chuckled, leaning his arm on the edge of the table. He only had to shift a little and already she was appreciating his thick, tousled black locks and begging herself to run a finger down his chiselled jawline.

Get a grip.

"So, where are you from? London? Around here?" she persisted after mentally scolding herself.

"Around here, Birmingham," he replied, anxious how far she'd dig. He hadn't really thought of a good cover story.

Claire pulled her hair into a tight ponytail. "Oh, nice. And what brings you into my flat?"

"You."

She rolled her eyes. "Does that actually work?"

"Pretty much," Zack confessed, grinning from ear to ear. "You're proving to be a difficult customer, however." And there was that boyish charm.

Claire snorted, standing up as she began to collect the dishes. "Since when was I a paying customer, *Romeo*?" She placed the dishes into the bowl, squirting the washing liquid and releasing hot water, watching as the suds expanded.

"*O, speak again, bright angel! for thou art as glorious to this night, being o'er my head!*" Zack rejoiced. He pushed his right arm out as if to reach for her, then tugged on his grey jogger's waistband, playing with the elastic string, while all the while an *irritating* grin lingered on his lips.

Claire's right brow lifted cynically. "All right, *Shakespeare*, calm down.

"Ah, ah, ah, where do you think you're going?" she scolded suddenly, hearing his naked feet plod away on the white linoleum floor. "I'm not doing all this washing up. You can at least do the drying!" she called out after him.

"I've got work to do," he replied, "but I'll be back in a second."

Seconds later, she felt two arms slithering around her waist, each fingertip burning into her skin. She could feel a hardened torso, firm thighs pressing against the back of her own. Gently, she felt hands slide towards her hips, furiously tugging them against his own. Her lips parted gently, her wrinkled, wet hands squeezed the sponge between them in the washing bowl as his hands wandered towards her breasts.

"Tell me what you what me to do," he whispered *against her ear.*

"Everything," she confessed.

Eagerly, she turned, mouth-to-mouth, soap suds crawling through her fingers into his hair. Tongues battling, no winner or loser, hands travelling skin-to-skin. The restless urge succumbing both bodies into one. A moan. A gasp.

Claire blinked. Another presence was noticeably absent.

She was standing at the sink; her hands were madly squeezing the sponge and a piece of pasta was bathing on top of a carpet of soap in the washing bowl. Either she had been caught day-dreaming or she was going completely crazy. *Claire preferred the latter.*

It was no surprise then when Zack, her newfound

roommate, returned, holding a laptop under his right arm, heading for the kitchen table, that she'd nearly kicked herself. *Don't even dare,* she threatened herself. What? *Those kissable lips she'd seconds ago only imagined tangoing with her own. Or his arms? Wrapped around her?* Nope.

"You look like you've seen a ghost," he remarked, setting his laptop down and switching the ON button.

"N-No," she said, swallowing at least a mouthful of saliva. "I'm just tired. Do you think you could help after you're done?" she hinted, exhaling afterwards, at his transfixed state towards the laptop screen.

Zack was too busy typing away to have heard.

***

ZACK

There was one thing he was afraid to leave untouched—and that was ensuring his plans go full steam ahead on the Brownfield Project, constructing renewable energy efficient homes, was in the green. Now, why was this important? Well, if anyone knew Zack's father, Elijah, he was a man of profit, a man even Zack believed had done corrupt business, paid the odd officer to look the other way, or evaded tax by some clever accounting. He'd seen it. Heck, his father had dodgy relations with a lieutenant in the police force, who'd personally ensured Zack's brother, Jared, that he wouldn't be convicted for underage drinking and driving. The point was, Zack knew that if his father heard he was making plans to alter the company's path, it would release Satan, himself, from hell. So, why had he agreed to Kyle's bet? He couldn't just blame his own competitive spirit. At first, it did appear silly. Yet what was more apparent was he could work alongside those researching the potential clientele market, estimate profits, and potentially sell his idea closer than he could as CEO. He wanted the research and drafting to be done to the highest standard, enough so he could impress the chairman of the board, whom he suspected was still under the high influence of his father.

"Zack?" she'd repeated for the fourth time, grasping his attention once he'd hit "send" on the email and attachment he'd needed Olivia, his personal assistant, to forward out.

"Yes?"

"Here," she said, throwing over a tea-towel.

"What's this?" he asked, catching it in his one hand.

"Well, we *call* this a towel. And what that means is you're supposed to get off your ass and help me dry up these plates. I think I deserve that, don't you?" she answered, holding a hand on her hip.

Zack licked his bottom lip, shutting his laptop lid down as he got to his feet. He'd hoped it wouldn't have come down to this. How on earth does one *dry up?* Not trying to sound thick or beyond helpless, but not once had he been told to *dry up.*

"C'mon," she encouraged, passing him a plate. "They aren't gonna dry themselves."

He shuffled his feet over, taking the plate from

her hand. Glancing at the tea-towel, he swallowed, then naturally assuming it was the same as drying oneself, he slowly patted the plate. He'd only begun and already she was passing him another from the pile.

Claire glanced over when she noticed the second plate hadn't been collected from her hand. "Have you even dried a plate before?" she asked, sighing.

"Yes, of course. I'm…just overly cautious to make sure it is indeed dry," he replied, squinting his eyes as he patted around the edges of the plate slowly. Claire chuckled.

"Move over, slow-coach," she demanded, taking the plate and towel from his hands. "We'll be all night. And I need sleep," she added, quickly swabbing the plate, putting it on the table, and taking the next one from the pile.

"Well, you've just forced me out of a job," he said.

CHAPTER FIVE

CLAIRE

Last night was *something*. Not a blink of sleep. She'd felt sweaty and was so thirsty that she got up six times just for a glass of water. It was possibly why she was slowly drowning herself in caffeine at seven o'clock in the morning.

She cuddled her fingers around the mug, exhaling as she stretched her toes a little and sat back in the kitchen chair, closing her eyes.

"Well, someone looks exhausted. Rough sleep?" She heard a fruity laugh skipping into the kitchen.

"Eurgh, pleeeeeeeease," she grumbled in a flat, dead tone. She slowly sat up, blinking quickly, as she couldn't comprehend the half-naked man in pyjama bottoms standing at the table. *He appeared to have forgotten his shirt once again*, she thought sarcastically. His chest was nearly bare of hair—except, she noticed, where the strands led downward from his belly button to the hidden places below.

"You really didn't get any, did you?" He smirked, rubbing his shoulder. His arm lifted just enough to get a glance at his curly black underarm hair. Why she was finding that so mildly attractive?

"No," she sighed, shaking her head. "Why are you up, anyway?"

"Work."

"Oh. I'd just presumed—"

"In fact," he interjected as he pulled out a bottle of milk from the fridge, "a little birdie told me we'll be seeing each other a lot more regularly."

Claire frowned, sitting up. "What?"

"You'll see soon," he said as he opened the top cupboard.

"Cornflakes are in the other one," she told him before that quizzical expression consumed her face once more. "I'm so confused."

"I get it," he said, shrugging his shoulders. "It's a lot to take in. After all, look at me. I'd dig me." The right corner of his lip tugged upwards.

"There's a mirror in the bathroom. Go ahead," she snorted.

"Do you mind lending a hand, though?" he replied humourlessly.

Claire rolled her eyes as she slowly got up. "Well, I'm using the shower, and you're doing whatever. If you're gonna enjoy yourself, don't make a mess."

So far, so good. Considering she'd allowed a god-like man into her apartment, she hadn't *cracked* as of *yet*. There was that odd daydream, and the inevitable staring, but where was she supposed to look when two ol' mean pair of pecs were on display? Now, showering. Her best option was to take her clothes in with her, in case she happened to come face-to-face with him.

Was it strange seeing men's shampoo and body wash stacked around the bathtub? It had not even been a day and already she was feeling like she'd been living with this man for half a century. And what was all this? See him regularly? She hoped he'd be out of her hair all day.

Claire dropped her towel and clothes onto the side, took out her razor from the mini cabinet above the towel rack, then stopped short. *Really?* Either she was imagining it, or that *fella* had the audacity to leave the toilet seat up. *Men,* she scoffed to herself, pinching the edge of the seat and putting it down slowly.

***

ZACK

Zack was sat on the sofa, quickly typing yet another email, so far, to Olivia, briefly bringing her up-to-date on his whereabouts. Under what seemed like a professional move, not a silly bet with Kyle, he'd prodded her to temporarily file him as an employee working under Sales and Marketing. That was one obstacle out of the way.

"Well, I don't know about you," Claire piped up. He shut his laptop down immediately, glancing over his right shoulder as she entered the living room. "But I'm going to work soon. So, yeah, I'll see you later or something."

"Actually, hold your horses. I'll get changed," he replied, sliding his laptop under the blue cushion and standing up.

"What?"

"Slide aside." He gestured. "Wait by the front door, and I'll meet you there," he instructed before walking towards the bedroom he had claimed.

Claire's nose wrinkled as she turned on her boot's heel, wondering what on earth he was on about. "What do you mean? I don't understand!" she called out.

"One second, sugarbun," he hollered.

"What did you just call me?" she snapped.

It was only seconds before he returned, dressed from head to toe in a dark navy shirt and grey trousers. "I said sugarbun," he said, ignoring her completely as he sat down on the sofa to tie his shoelaces.

"Errr, no, no." She wiggled her index finger, stomping right in front of him. "We are not on a nickname basis," she said.

"Sorry, sugar," he replied, distracted as he lifted his other shoe onto the coffee table and began to tie that lace up.

"Did you just hear me?" she grumbled. "And look, if you're implying that you're getting the same bus as me, then hurry up, because I need to get to work."

"I could do with a coffee before we go," Zack confessed, dropping his hands onto his knees.

"Go make it yourself." Claire frowned.

"I would, but I'm still getting used to the kitchen," he said innocently.

Claire rolled her eyes.

"Thanks." Zack grinned with a hint of mischief as he took the mug from Claire's hands.

Claire frowned, looking elsewhere.

He brought it to his lips, swallowing only a mouthful before he spat it out.

"Eurgh, what is this?" he complained. "It tastes like salt."

"Oh, *dear*," Claire mocked, holding her hands up to her either side of her cheeks. "I must have accidentally put salt instead of sugar in your coffee."

Zack hesitated, his eyes full of scrutiny. "Accidents happen," he muttered, aware she'd deliberately spiked his drink for added measure of revenge.

***

CLAIRE

"Are you following me?" she hissed, speed walking as she noticed he was hot on her heels. Not only had he caught the same bus, sat behind her, persistently bugged her, he'd also got off at the same stop, refusing all the while to answer her question of where he was going.

"Nope," he said, following her up the pavement to the reception.

"Err, yes, you are," she meekly squealed, jabbing her hand towards him as he followed behind her through the glass doors.

"Nope." He shook his head. "Don't know what

you're talking about."

Claire stopped dead in her tracks. Irritated now, she was about to stomp right up to him when he took her hand and dragged her towards him.

"What are you—"

Zack pulled her close to his side once he stopped them at the reception desk. "Morning, lovely." He smiled towards the receptionist, who pinked up, flustered. "I'm Zack Chase. New employee. I need a temporary pass until my card comes through. There should be an email on that lovely computer of yours," he explained.

Claire was gobsmacked. He was working here? And second, why was she still gripping his hand? Claire immediately slid out of it, frowning at his gorgeous face as he carried on flirting obnoxiously with the receptionist, whose face resembled a bloody tomato.

"Thanks," he replied, eagerly taking the pass out of her hands after she'd done her homework.

As soon as they were out of earshot, Claire hissed, "Since when do you work here? And what gave you the right to pull me like that? I'm not some sort of ragdoll."

"It was for moral support," Zack said, ignoring her fury as he advanced on through the barriers and onwards to the lobby of lifts.

"Moral support, my ass! You practically dragged me across that floor. Who do you think you are?" she argued, tucking a flyaway of hair behind her ear and watching as he pressed the button several times to call the lift.

"Zack Chase," he replied, shrugging his

shoulders.

They entered the lift then, squeezing into the small gap amongst the several other people congregated all around. It took another five minutes before they reached their floor after stopping at every one. Thank God she hadn't been shoved into him. It was already enough frustration knowing he was not only living under her roof, but was working here too.

Claire breathed a sigh of relief as she exited the lift but almost immediately sucked it back in seeing Zack, her roommate, barely an acquaintance, step out too. She would have said something if it wasn't for Graves heading on over.

"Ah, I presume you're Zack Chase," Graves said, glancing briefly at the paperwork in his hands. "Do forgive me. I've only just received all this." He tucked it under his right arm before offering his hand out. "Clive Graves. Department boss." He smiled, shaking Zack's hand. "Wait." He paused as his smile lingered a little. "Have we met before?"

Zack swallowed. "No, I don't think so."

"Ah." Graves shook his head. "I must be mistaking you for somebody else. Anyway, what a coincidence that you've happened to stumble in with Claire Winter. I would have introduced you to Monica, but she's absent this morning. She's my leading second," he informed Zack. "Anyway, I've assigned you to Claire for this week. You don't mind, do you, Claire?"

Claire felt like a fly, a fly being eaten by a frog. It was like a never-ending list of cock-ups. First, she'd invited some conceited, pretty boy into her apartment, who apparently works here now, and Graves assigned his ass to her for a week.

"I know you'll do it well," he said confidently, then he glanced at his wrist watch. "Oh, yes. Could you be a star and do these? I don't think Monica's confident enough yet, and I know you'll be able to look these over." He passed over a red file, "Sales and Marketing" imprinted boldly on the flap. "And terrible news on the promotion, Claire. My office is always available if you need to talk." He turned around and walked off to his office.

She could have crumpled up that file in her hands. Oh, she was feeling every inch of her skin burn with anger.

"What promotion?" Zack asked. He scanned the file in her hands, vaguely interested.

"A promotion I *should* have had," she snapped. "What does he even think he's doing? He's taking me as a mug. I should have had that promotion, not doing fucking Monica's work."

"Well, why didn't you get it?"

Claire sighed. "Ask her who's been sharing her pillows at night." She adjusted the strap on her bag, preparing to head on over to her desk.

"Claire!" Darren came out the office's kitchen, holding a mug in his right hand, simmering all too soon as he caught a glimpse of Zack standing next to her. "H-hey," he began, at a loss for words. "I've been looking for you all morning."

"Sorry, we got caught up," she mumbled. "I'm just gonna set Zack up, and I'll join you in a bit. I could do with something to drink."

He nodded, hesitantly shuffling back to the

kitchen.

"Well, looks like I'm never going to have a break from you," she confessed.

Zack chuckled lightly. "And that's a problem?"

She didn't answer, resuming her trek to her cubicle at the far end of the office, opposite two gigantic windows open to the city skyline. Claire knew he was following her because about three females turned in their seats, glancing at *something* or *somebody*.

She dropped her bag onto the desk. "Okay, well, I suppose you'll be sharing my desk for the time being until I'm confident enough I can leave you on your own," she said, then she began sliding sticky notes, her notepad, and pencil pot to the side to make enough room. "I should probably get you a chair."

Claire took off to the front, knowing the office pushed spares up there if they weren't being used. She'd grabbed one easily, pushing the wheels back, but wanted to stop when she saw Monica, who was *supposedly* absent, near her desk, nipping at Zack already like a shark. *Of course,* she thought. *Who else?*

She could already smell the excessive lavender perfume Monica wore. That she-devil was *literally* giggling like a fairy, teasing her hand on Zack's chest as he grinned triumphantly.

"I'm sure we could arrange something *soon*," he said, running his fingertips across his perfectly sharp stubbled jawline.

"I'm sure we will," Monica's soft, irritatingly high-pitched voice buzzed. Claire tensed with frustration. How she wanted to throw a punch! This woman could prance about all she liked without a thought of worry, and here Claire was, doing her work. Oh, and *now* her roommate was being lured into her web.

Claire's eyes daggered into Monica's back as she sashayed off.

"So," she heard Zack sigh. "Is she that office slut?"

It took Claire by surprise.

"*Figures*," he continued, sitting down on the desk chair she'd brought over. "She's desperate as they get. No wonder he wouldn't be able to resist."

"Yeah, well, she's supposed to be walking you through all this. It's in her new contract. But..." Claire shrugged her shoulders. "I'm doing it. So let's just get the basics over and done with." She sat down in her own chair, set up the computer, and began. "So, as you know, we have a marketing and sales team. *Only*...I do both, not by choice. Graves like to pile on the work, so prepare for a shit ton of it."

***

ZACK

Zack nodded, distracted by her lips. They were hypnotic. Each syllable produced seemed to dance right off her tongue. Was he going crazy? Or he was beginning to see animated rabbits, birds, and even a fucking deer congregate in the background? He blinked. Now, the rabbits were *fucking*. Great. He wasn't that horny. It had been less than two days. She cleared her throat. "Zack, did you get that?"

He nodded, trance-like again. There was a complete forest of animals now.

Claire sighed. "Well, I'm going to leave you to it now. When I come back, I expect you to have at least highlighted the sales data in this spreadsheet that needs attention. Okay?"

***

CLAIRE

She got up, then headed to the kitchen.

Darren was soon on her case. "So? So? What was it like?"

"What was what like?" she asked, switching on the kettle. "What? How Graves is being a complete jerk and making me do all Monica's work? Or the fact I've got some pretty boy living under my roof and now he works here too?"

Darren rolled his eyes, shuffling around the table as he eagerly swept up to her side. "Noooo, not any of that," he muttered, squeezing his hands on her shoulder. "What was he like? Did he do you good?"

"Darren! We did not have…sex," she hissed, shaking his hands off her shoulder before reaching for the teabags out of the overhead cupboard.

He whined, "I was hoping you did. How could you just not, though? Look at the guy. You could be a power couple."

Claire snorted, stirring her cup of tea. "No, I don't think so."

She spent another ten minutes lounging about with Darren before she decided it was best she got on ahead with that work Graves had piled on her, and she did need to check if Zack had done as he was told. As if she hadn't enough on her case, she had to babysit the exact person she was hoping she wouldn't have to see until evening.

There was no Zack. And three or four rows had been highlighted at best. Claire could have screamed.

"Really?" She frowned.

No sign of him whatsoever. Nor did she have the strength to want to go find him. Instead, she sat down, minimised the spreadsheet, and began trying to get through her own work.

Half an hour passed. Zack turned up. *Only* he wasn't alone. She'd seen him exiting Graves' office, Monica trailing behind him. Claire would have brushed it off if she suspected Graves was also in there, but she'd seen the man wandering off earlier. So there were two options: either he— scratch that, this was Monica they were talking about. She'd slept with nearly half the male population in the department, even some married men.

"Sorry, I got a bit caught up," she heard Zack apologise as he came over and sat down. She ignored him.

"Claire?"

Her fingers stomped on each individual letter on the keyboard.

"Claire?"

"What?" she snapped. She saw Darren, opposite

her, peek his head over the cubicle for a brief second before sinking back down to his chair.

"Are you okay? I've said your name about three times, and you didn't respond," he replied, a weak smile still lingering across his lips. He was also obnoxiously playing with the red stapler, adding one more thing to the list of things that were bugging her.

"Okay? Okay? Pssf, sure." She rolled her eyes, then dragged the spreadsheet back onto the screen. "Where were you? You did barely anything I asked. What, were you making yourself at home?" she said with exasperation.

"I was asked…and making myself at home? What's that supposed to mean?" he asked, rubbing his chin as he put the stapler down.

"You know perfectly well," Claire hissed.

"Wait," he frowned, "you think—you think I was messing about with that Monica?"

She didn't respond and instead chose to turn in her seat and pretend to read a sheet.

"You do, don't you?" A dry laugh left his lips.

Once again, she chose not to reply.

"First, I think I made myself very clear I wasn't interested. And two." He paused, leaning in closer. "Even if I did, what's it to you? You jealous or something?"

Claire gasped and turned in her seat. "No way. I would never be jealous. I barely even know you, and I'm already convinced you're some pretty boy thinking he can have his way with every woman," she hissed.

"Sure."

Claire picked up a blue highlighter from her pot of pens. "I'm *not* jealous. I'm annoyed because you haven't done anything. You're such a—"

"A what?" he interjected, running the pad of his thumb across a pen, rolling it back and forth along the desk.

"A jerk!" she hissed quietly, aggressively highlighting a passage of text on the paper in front of her.

"That's sweet," he replied with a plastered smile.

"Eurgh," she groaned, slapping the highlighter down. "Could you not smile, just for a second? Or even speak? I'd really appreciate it. Thank you," she added, picking the highlighter back up.

"Honestly, it's okay. I get it. Jealousy is just your thing," he remarked. She could smell the heavy stench of his cologne intruding her personal space as he leaned in. She frowned further when he stood up.

"Where do you think you're going now?" she complained. "You can't just get up. You're supposed to be finishing off this spreadsheet." She brought the sheet back up on the computer screen.

Zack didn't say a word. He smiled, then walked off. Claire switched on like a red traffic light. She pursued him, hot on his heels as he headed through the stairwell door. She'd had enough. *Who did he think he was?* she thought as she pushed open the door.

"Now—" She stopped midway as he grasped her hand and swiftly drew her towards the wall adjacent to the steel banister on the left. He then clasped her other hand and held them to the sides of her hips as he closed the space between them. She was startled and a little dazed. She wasn't entirely willing to push him off. Her heart sped up, erratic like a set of drums.

"It's okay to be jealous...but do you really think I would have?" he whispered, a low growl at the back of his throat accompanying that smug grin beaming like the Northern lights.

"I don't care what you do," she hissed, trying to shuffle her wrists from his hands. "I just wanted you to have done the work. And besides," she narrowed her eyes, "why would I be jealous? You ain't nothing special." Smugness seemed to radiate off him, because every second he just seemed to grow more and more with glee.

Zack chuckled, low and gravelly. "Oh, that's where you know you're wrong, *sweetheart*." He slowly let loose of her right hand, an opportunity that she could easily have used to nudge him away, but Claire remained where she was, pressing her lips together, hesitant. Her eyes interrogated his.

His fingers caressed the naked surface of her cheek. Each tiny, invisible hair was attracted like a fish to a hook. She could have told him to stop, but she didn't. It was mad. She was going mad. Either this space was suddenly getting hotter or her core was burning with sudden desire. And it didn't help she was becoming consumed in that cloud of strong, spicy cologne that tickled her nostrils.

Claire bit down on her tongue. She felt his hand glide effortlessly towards her lower thigh, climb up beneath her dress, and briskly touch the edge of her knickers. She could have stopped him, but she didn't, and she wasn't going to.

***

ZACK

Aggressively, he locked his body close, searching her eyes for an answer, *anything.* An answer for himself. A sexual frustration. He needed her to push him away. Zack felt like a lion, caged up, begging to be released. *It was just all too inappropriate,* he thought. He'd only just met the woman, and already he had her against the wall. How on earth was this all gonna play out?.

He was stiffening.

She didn't, nor did his conscience, convince him enough to stop. He leaned in and kissed her warm lips, embracing the gentle touch matching his own. He dared to further test the waters, nipping his front teeth on her bottom lip before retracting back. She didn't say a word. It must have been a literal second until she surprised him by slamming her lips to his. It was like igniting a fire, because once she'd slid her arms around his thick, strong neck, he had her pinned to the wall like no tomorrow. Her mouth, sweet and hot against his, voluntarily parted, colliding their tongues in a battle. Urgency built as his hands greedily grabbed her ass cheeks, pressing her core closer to his stiff bulge screaming to be let out. And whilst she scavenged through his black forest of hair, she was obviously enjoying how his tongue danced to the back of her throat.

Claire sank into his arms as he tore his mouth

away, gathering much needed oxygen despite how his heart gnawed with hunger and his dick swelled with lust.

"No! No! No!" Claire yelped, slapping her right hand to her mouth. She shook her head in utter shame as she slid away from him, abruptly breaking the chain. "That did not just happen. I did not. I did not. Fuck! Fuck! No! No!"

"Well, you could have fooled me," Zack croaked, his voice dipping, slightly offended by her reaction. He'd never had any woman react as disgusted as that before.

"That was a huge mistake. That shouldn't have happened," she mumbled, ignoring him as she paced the landing and remained a good distance away from him.

"Gee, a mistake? I think you'll find your tongue was also halfway down my throat," he said, watching as she continued to pace and curse under her breath.

Claire stopped dead, hissing as she covered her eyes. "Do you mind?"

Zack looked down. Not like he needed to. He knew he was hard.

"Fucks' sake," Claire cried, dropping her hands. "Eurgh! This is your fault. Why did you kiss me? God, I hate you."

Zack shuffled the band of his trousers. "Good, because I hate you then," he replied.

"I hated you first," she chided childishly.

"Well, I hate you more," he responded, distracting his hand elsewhere to calm his persistent friend.

***

CLAIRE

"Eurgh! Let—let's just not ever speak about this. You go do whatever, and I'm going to the bathroom," she instructed, running her hands through her hair as she headed for the door.

Thank God, if anything, the tiny four-by-four window obstructed any wandering eyes.

Eventually she did return, holding her head high, shoulders raised forward, hoping she was fooling everyone as she trekked to her cubicle. He was sat there. Not like she expected anyone else to be in that seat. He must have sensed her nearby because he soon sat up, coolly smiling as he turned his head.

"Don't say a word," she hissed, sitting down and pulling the chair in.

"I wasn't going to," he replied ever so innocently, resting his leg across his knee and rocking gently back in the chair. Then he stopped, sat forward, and picked up a piece of paper. "In fact, I was just lending my expertise to this beauty. Whatever you feel is purely your own doing," he teased.

"Oh, shut up," she hissed, snatching the paper from him. "Let me have a look." Claire sighed before concentrating on the figures before her.

"Looks like renewability is possible? I see those figures on that trial run could potentially be a point of growth," Zack suggested, interested in what she thought.

Claire sighed. "Yes. Maybe. Only last month's

investment wasn't exactly enough. The board apparently isn't all hand-in-hand with the scheme. The CEO is supposed to be announcing something very soon."

"Oh, is he? Do…you perhaps—or have you ever met this—"

"No," she interjected, then she snorted. "Just because we're in the same building, it doesn't mean Mr. Fancy Pants comes down. He's like old or something. Now, stop messing with that stapler, it's bugging me." She slapped his hand gently away from the device. "Although," she piped up, folding her arms as she looked ahead of her. "I'm tempted to fight my case over this promotion. I mean, surely the CEO could hear my side of the story, considering I'm babysitting your ass as well as other work," she scoffed.

"Babysitting? No, *darling*. We could have been up to so much more—"

"Ah, ah, what did I say?" she whispered, nudging his shoulder. "No more on that. Now, shut up and read some of these out while I fill them out on the spreadsheet. That will give you something useful to do," she ordered, slapping the sheet full of figures onto his lap. "Now, read." She hovered her fingers over the keyboard.

***

ZACK

His tone felt robotic as he read out percentages and numbers as she typed them out. It only became a joy when their little activity was interrupted by some stranger lingering by Claire's chair.

"Hey," he heard the male specimen speak, who looked as if he was already stiffening in his boxers. *Who is this dork?* Zack thought.

Claire turned. "Oh, hey, Jason," she said. "What's up?"

"I'm just seeing if you're all set for Saturday. I hear there's good movies on—scary, and you know, comedy." He smiled, reddening ever so slightly within the apples of his cheeks.

Zack sat up, narrowing his eyes at the fella.

"Yeah, that's fine," she replied. "Just remind me in the morning or something by text. I can sometimes be a sloth and sleep in till dusk if I'm not careful," she joked.

"Will do." He laughed lightly, sticking his index finger out as he jabbed it toward her. *What a fool,* Zack thought. *Way to embarrass yourself.*

Then he began to walk off, hesitant at the end of the aisle whether he was going to sit down or not.

"Would you stop staring?" she snapped at Zack.

Zack leaned back in. "So, what's his deal?"

"None of your business kind of deal."

"I could make it my business if I provide him details about how my tongue was thrust down the back of your throat—"

"Zack!" she growled. "You wouldn't dare."

"Why? You look ever so flustered, *love.* Want me to get the fire extinguisher?" he replied, teasing her with another one of those flirtatious grins.

Claire wanted to punch that perfectly structured, God-given face of his and send it packing to the moon. He was beginning to get on her nerves.

"J-Just, let's get back on with this work, please?" she asked, pointing her finger at the sheet laid out in front of him.

***

"Err, where do you think you're going?" Claire interrogated as he stood up.

"The men's bathroom…would you like to join me?" A faint smile toyed on his lips.

He was lying about that. In fact, he just wanted to get away from that work. Although, he had the most important job of all—signing off deals and leading the company in the right direction. *Well, what he was supposed to be able to do?* His employees had the pain-in-the-butt task of actually carrying out his actions in depth.

Zack was walking on ahead when Graves rudely stepped in front of him, urgently heading through the emergency stairwell and climbing up a flight of stairs. Call Zack nosey, but he became rather suspicious of his behaviour. Of course, he was cautious to follow, just stopping below as he heard the man begin to speak.

"Yes, I-I know, I know. This Tuesday. Yes," he muttered. "Please, just hold your horses. It's really tricky business. I don't see you risking your job for this." Zack's interest grew.

Zack heard no more and took that as a sign he was finished with the call. His behaviour intrigued him, but he couldn't exactly do any further investigation if he didn't know what he was on about. He left quietly, returning to the office, and headed back to his cubicle.

Before he even placed a toe inside, someone grabbed his arm with tremendous grip and pulled him through a door. It must have been a stockroom from the sight of pencil pots, pens, and stacks of paper on steel shelves.

"Can I help you?" he asked, humour laced in his tone.

"Let's just get something straight here, *buddy.* I do *not,* and I *repeat,* do not find you at all attractive. It is the opposite," Claire said, holding her hands on her hips. "That kiss was a mistake. I want to make this clear. If you breathe a word to anyone, and I mean *anyone,* I will personally cut your dick off," she hissed. The white light above blared against the top of her head, adding a fierceness that was spitting off her tongue.

"*Honey,*" Zack exhaled. "You wouldn't want that. You want my dick. But I accept your apology."

"Since when did that sound at all like an apology? That was a warning!" she spat, jabbing her finger at him.

"*But* you don't deny it." He smiled, leaning on the side of the shelf.

"Eurghhh!" she moaned, throwing her hands up in the air. "You're so conceited!"

"It's just confidence."

"Arrogance, that's what it is." She rolled her eyes. "It has no effect upon me at all," she muttered, her eyes deadly serious.

Zack leaned back up off the shelf and moved closer, just enough that his body was inches from hers. "Oh, yeah," he challenged, the sweetened smell of her perfume enveloping them.

"Yeah," she said, stepping forward. "Now, I suggest you get your ass back into that office and get on with that work, *buddy*. Because as you can see, you don't affect me at all," she added, folding her arms triumphantly.

He raised his right eyebrow. Without a single word, he moved forward, pushing her gently back. Her spine contacted an old, brown cupboard plastered with stickers. She knew his game from the sight of hunger glinting in the corner of his eyes. Claire held her position; she tried to remain calm even as his hand slapped gently above her head on the wall.

"You *sure*?" he asked quietly, searching her eyes, just like he'd managed to do earlier.

***

CLAIRE

Claire pressed her lips together. No way was she kissing this man twice. She hadn't meant to in the first place. She stood up more firmly and pushed her hand gently on his chest. "You're a bit desperate, aren't you?" she replied, sliding aside. "You need to calm yourself, *pal*," she added, suddenly alarming Zack as she tugged on his belt loop. "Keep it in your pants," she advised. Then without another word, she walked out of the stockroom, leaving him a little stunned.

Darren was on the other side of the stockroom

door. He sported a massive grin, as if he'd just won an Oscar. At first, Claire presumed he was just happy to see her, but that soon was flushed down the toilet as she heard Zack coming out from behind her.

"Hello, nice to meet you. I'm Zack," he introduced himself to Darren.

CHAPTER SIX

CLAIRE

Why had she kissed him back? It had been running through Claire's mind for the past four hours. Thankfully, she had the apartment to herself; Zack was out and about that evening. She sat on the sofa, legs propped up to the side of her as she held a glass of fizzy pop in her hand, bored with what was on television. Each time she closed her eyes, she could picture their lips smacked together. *Why?* What had driven her to do it? She had every chance to push him away.

The television screen flipped to TV ads, something she tried to focus on to distract her mind. It wasn't working. The man talking about PPI suddenly distorted into Zack's face. "PPI...Claire, *want a kiss?*" it was saying, startling Claire, who blinked about a dozen times. She was genuinely going crazy, wasn't she?

Darren hadn't thought so; he already had it wrapped up in his head that they were seemingly rocking about together. Her and Zack? *No way!* It was merely a mistake. Maybe she was sexually frustrated; she'd rather believe that than think it was because she was attracted to that horrific man!

Why did she deserve all this? First the promotion and now this guy? Was she getting punished or something?

Outside, she could hear sudden commotion, honking horns and the odd shouting. She got up and headed towards the blinds, opening them to see what all the fuss was about. It was heaving with rain, bouncing off the roofs of stationary cars; it was like an orchestra of metallic sound. Three or four vehicles queued up one after the other, the *cause,* some stumbling fool crossing the road. Claire rolled her eyes, *some drunk idiot.* He was walking side to side, mindless to the traffic around him. She couldn't help but pity the figure; not one person from the cars had offered to help. She was very much tempted to go out herself until she saw them manage to get across and lean heavily on a sign post.

Claire closed the blinds and headed back for the couch. At least it was more interesting to witness than the dry commercial showing on the telly of someone selling laundry detergent.

BANG!

She jumped nearly out of her skin. Zack was leaning through the front door, his black locks wet and sticking to the front of his forehead.

"Zack?" she said, confused as she got to her feet and threw the controller down onto the sofa. It appeared the figure who had struggled to cross that road moments ago had been him. She hurried over, instantly absorbed in the slap of alcohol reeking off him. "Have you been drinking?" she complained, huffing as she felt the weight of his right arm slump over her shoulder.

"Fuck, I have," he croaked, wriggling his finger about briefly before dropping it to his side. "I swear…I only…" he hiccupped, "…had a…few."

"You sure smell like you've had plenty," she replied, leading him steadily to the sofa and gently helping him down. "You're gonna catch a cold if we don't take these wet clothes off you." She hurried to the bathroom to fetch a towel.

He groaned; she could hear him shuffling, clearly struggling with something.

"Ay, ay," she nagged as she returned, putting the dark blue towel on the arm of the single chair. "Don't go falling asleep on me yet. We need to take these clothes off," she groaned as she struggled to lift him up forward. "C'mon," she urged, huffing and puffing. For a man of his size, he sure weighed a ton. Eventually, she got him to sit forward with effort as he kept wanting to lunge back.

She stripped off his leather jacket, then his shirt, unbuttoning each individual white button until Mr. Mean Pecs made another show. *How convenient,* she thought. A terrible habit not to want to stare. Even a graze of her fingertips against his skin sent her into overload. *Ridiculous!*

"Okay, nearly done," she muttered, mainly to reassure herself.

"Hey, *Claire,*" he managed to say after another series of hiccups.

81

"Yes?"

"You're…not g-gonna…really cho-opp off my dick, are you?" he slurred.

She rolled her eyes. "No, Zack." She grabbed the towel and wrapped it around his shoulders; thankful it hid *most* of the glorious naked canvas. "Now, lie back. We need to take these trousers off. You can sort your…*boxers,* yourself," she told him. He gently sat back, his eyes still sealed shut as she attempted to slide the ends off. This was so, so, so, *not good,* she thought as she realised with much thought that they weren't gonna budge without undoing the button. *Really.* She looked up to the ceiling. Someone was doing this on purpose. She could have left him in the trousers and sent him to bed, but they were wet, not exactly comfortable to sleep in, or he could catch a cold.

She breathed in. *You got this,* she encouraged, *quick scoop in.*

Slowly, she leaned her fingers in. *Bloody hell,* she scolded herself. *This isn't like rocket science or building a car. Hurry up with it.* Then she met the icy, cold kiss of the trouser button and with haste undid it. The band of his boxers peeked and only grew taller and taller as she pulled down the trousers. *Mother O' Mercy.* She swallowed. *Big or what?*

Claire stood up, diverting her eyes elsewhere as she took the discarded trousers into her arms. "Right," she coughed. "Erm, we gotta get you up to bed now, Zack." He was awkwardly sound asleep, unaware, the *near-enough* treacherous boundary that she had to cross to prevent *him* from catching a cold. It didn't appear he was even going to lift a finger. Would Claire even manage to pick him up and take him to his bed? She decided to leave him there. Claire guided him to lie down before propping the red blanket over him and positioning the grey mop bucket beneath him on the floor, in case. Then she returned with a glass of water, placing it on the coffee table.

She sighed as she picked up his leather jacket, startled at the sight of a fifty-pound note fleeting from the inner pocket. *Gee,* she thought, *someone's doing well.* She slid it back in and took it into the kitchen. It was dawning eleven, so she left them on the side, deciding she had enough drama for one day. *He'd also better have a goddamn good excuse in the morning.* She sighed inwardly, turning off the lamp light.

***

CLAIRE

Ah, blissful. There it is again. That groaning alarm clock. She hit the snooze button, instantly killing its urgent call. Exhaling, Claire spread out her arms, confused as her right hand met a hard-ish but soft surface. *What?* Her fingertips traced the outline, wondering what on earth she was following. *Huh?* Hang on. Now, it felt fleshy.

Claire turned her head.

"Ow!" someone moaned. "Knock it off!"

"What are you doing in my bed?" she exclaimed, jumping up to her feet as if she'd just seen a mouse

83

crawling along the carpet.

Zack groaned into the pillow he was desperately hugging. "Stop yelling! I need sleep. You're in…my bed, anyway. So, stop complaining."

"No, no, no," she objected, grabbing her pillow and slapping it on his back. "Get up! Get up!"

"Okay, okay," he said, defending himself as he held his arm to cover his face. He sat up gently, rubbing his forehead and still very much in the element of sleep. "What do you want? Can't you give a man some time to himself?"

"Not if he so happens to have waltzed right into my room. How did you get in? I left you in the living room," she replied, shaking her head as she dropped to her knees and glanced at her door, wondering if she'd locked her door last night.

He squinted. "I don't…know. I can't remember," he grumbled. "Now, can I go back to sleep, or do you need to take my fingerprints or something?"

"No, you certainly cannot. You're not going back to sleep in my bed, nor can you—you have work. Meaning, get your ass up, go sort yourself out, and I'll meet you in the kitchen," she ordered as she got up off her bed.

"Fine."

***

ZACK

A hot cloud of steam hugged his naked body as he stood in the bathtub, scrubbing his face.

He hadn't had time to reminisce. Yesterday was

a blur. He remembered kissing Claire, then heading to some local bar in town called *Ozone* and ordering three dozen or so dry liquors. He'd drowned himself. Listened to some fella's story about his cheating wife, then completely hammered himself into oblivion. Zack knew not why he got drunk, he'd thought of many excuses, but none seemed adequate.

Zack found Claire in the kitchen. Her hands cupped a mug as she read from a newspaper spread out on the white marble counter.

He cleared his throat.

"So, apologies. I had no intention of—"

"Getting drunk? Sleeping in my bed?" she interrupted, raising her right brow.

"Y-Yeah," he agreed, scratching the top of his head. "I mean, I wasn't exactly sober."

"Not that it's my business, but were you drunk for a reason?" she asked, knocking off the crumbs of toast that had fallen onto her red pencil skirt.

"No idea," he said truthfully.

"Genius."

There was silence as she turned back to the newspaper and he aimlessly looked around.

"Erm…so, I didn't say anything strange to you last night?" he queried, wondering if he had implied anything towards his real position, AKA *real identification.*

"No, you went asleep pretty quickly," she replied, passing him a mug of coffee.

A look of relief swept his face.

***

Zack was heavily fixated on the computer screen, scanning through the last year's spreadsheet.

Project 34 was his initial attempt to introduce the construction of renewable homes that would include recyclable water and waste, solar panels, mini wind turbines, insulation, and car sharing schemes. He was so passionate to see it as a reality that he had hired designers to sketch the plans, had the finance team estimate profits, and yet the corporation's board only managed under three percent investment. It said it *there, clear as day.*

"I don't understand," he muttered to himself, squinting at the figures on the screen.

"What don't you understand?" Claire asked. She had returned from the photocopier holding a fresh batch of printed paper in her arms. She placed them on the edge of the desk as she leaned forward, looking at the screen.

"I swear you've been looking at that all morning," she stated, ushering him to scoot his chair aside.

"Clive Graves looks over these, doesn't he?" he said, ignoring her previous comment.

"Yes, he has the final look before we archive them and have them sent down to the accounting and finance department," she replied as she reached for the stapler from his side of the desk.

"And the board only invested three percent?" Zack persisted.

"If that's what the figure said, then yes."

Zack was completely baffled. *Surely, this was a mistake?*

"Besides," she added, stapling several pieces of

paper together. "Why are you so drummed up about some old project? Do I need to be suspicious or something? Are you some company spy?"

Zack swallowed. "No, I'm just curious. I suppose...you could say I'm passionate about renewability. It just doesn't seem to add up, though. It's noted here." He pointed to the screen that held a text box detailing comments. "That there are potential clienteles within the market, and so it's recommended at a ten percent investment starting point. All follows until *here*, it's clearly calculated at three percent."

Claire leaned over to glance at the screen. "That's strange," she suggested, shrugging her shoulders.

"Yeah, but surely an accountant would have picked up on the miscalculation. Where's the seven percent gone?" he argued, vexed as he looked from the screen to Claire. He hadn't seen this copy. His was overtly different, plainly suggesting to him there was not enough interest in the housing crisis to go forth with these plans. *So how did ten percent go to three percent?* It wasn't like he could admit to Claire he had a copy that didn't mention the ten percent suggestion at all. Clearly, someone had manipulated this intentionally.

"Do you remember looking over this?" he asked, vaguely watching Claire as she stapled another handful of paper together before placing it on top of the neat stack.

"Erm, yeah, I suppose. I mean, marketing and sales did work alongside accounting. Like, I remember researching it, and I had recommended ten percent, but that's just one opinion out of the dozen in this department," she replied as she scratched the end of her nose. "Look, it's done and dusted now, so you might as well..." she paused as she leaned over to reach for the mouse, "...stop looking...over it." Then she clicked to exit the file.

Zack opened his mouth to say something but decided not to. He could see his behaviour was becoming rather obsessive, something that could question his behaviour. It didn't mean he wouldn't stop looking into Project 34. He was of the mind to head up to his office later and check his database to see if it matched what he suspected.

"Sorry," he muttered quietly, drumming his fingers anxiously upon the desk. "I was just curious. Anyway...pass us over that sheet then. I'll help you speed things up."

Lunch hour soon arrived; things between Claire and Zack hadn't been awkward at all. Work consumed their time together. He was also distracted. And Claire was desperately trying to finish *Monica's* work from the other day that Graves had kindly assigned her to do. So, she wasn't at all hot-headed, irritated, or wishing she had a butcher's knife and going all psycho on him, *no*—instead, Claire was calm and collected as she headed down to the café on the ground floor.

***

CLAIRE

Darren was scooping a handful of potato salad as

she placed her tray down next to his on the bar. His pink tongue was peeking from the right corner of his lip as he scooped some more—anyone would have thought he was meticulously etching serial numbers on a pair of diamonds.

"I'm starving," she complained, grabbing the large plastic spoon and shovelling it into the tomato pasta.

"For dick?" he teased.

Claire rolled her eyes. "You know how to wind me up, don't you?"

Darren chuckled as he slid his own tray down, following the queue of people heading for the cashiers. "You love me. Anyway, we need to talk."

"Why?"

"What do you mean why?"

"Yesterday. You, the stockroom, and that deliciously handsome roommate of yours," he said. He tucked his fingers into his trouser pocket as he clawed his brown wallet out.

"Nothing happened," she lied. "He was…just getting paper. And I was showing him where it was." *As if that sounded better, she thought.*

"Er, hm, whatever you say. Anyway, we could be discussing that date of yours this weekend," he insisted, handing over ten pounds to the cashier, who looked like she needed a hell of holiday somewhere in sunny Spain.

"It's not a date," Claire disagreed. "It's just—"

"You can't tell me it's not. I told you that Jason has always had something for you," he argued as they headed towards a four-seater table in the dead centre of the café. "Oh, and look!" He pointed.

"There he is now. Let's invite him, shall we?" He placed his tray down, then hurried across the space towards Jason, who appeared to be making up his mind over which sandwich to eat.

Claire could only roll her eyes. *As if two people, female and male, equated automatically to a date. It is not a date at all. It's just going to be a friendly gathering, two people just going to see a movie. No funny business.*

Darren was grinning ear to ear as he ushered Jason to their table. He didn't sit down. Instead, he picked up his red tray, gave her a wink, and then swung off in the other direction. Claire blinked, but she didn't exactly have enough time to digest what on earth Darren was scheming, considering Jason was sitting exactly opposite her, sheepishly smiling.

"Er, hi. Where did he go?" she asked, digging her fork into her pasta.

"Oh, he needed to finish off some work. He said you might need the company. So, here I am," he muttered, anxiously rubbing the palms of his hands together.

Of course he did, Claire thought.

Claire offered a polite smile and dug her fork back into the lettuce, hesitant, not knowing what to say next. He sat there aimlessly looking around, tapping his shoe incessantly against the floor.

"So, I'm just gonna come out with it. Is this weekend some sort of date?" she blurted, scanning every inch of his face to deduce what she needed to know.

"Erm—"

"Claire, there you are," someone interrupted.

She turned towards the voice, instantly sighing inside as Zack approached the table.

***

ZACK

He didn't feel the need to ask as he sat down on the chair and folded his arms loosely across the table.

"And you are?"

"Jason. We actually met—"

"So, anyway," Zack rudely interrupted once again. "I thought I'd be a pain and come pester my flatmate. The food looks a bit shit, don't you think?" He made a grimace at Claire's pasta.

"Flatmate?" Jason meekly muttered. He seemed to go pale in the face.

"Yes, but—"

"Did you know she snores? I mean, bloody hell, it's like I'm listening to a lawn mower twenty-four seven," Zack interrupted, again. He was irritating her beyond belief. She had a right mind to kick him under the table, but she refrained, opting to remain calm and collected.

Jason never said a word.

"She's terrible for space as well. She takes all the quilt."

Claire choked on air. "Oh, would you look at the time. I'm just going to er, yeah, go do some work. I'll see you later," she stuttered, standing hastily to her feet as she went for the escape.

As if by magic, *he,* out of all the people she had

hoped would stop pestering her, was right hot on her trail, leaving poor, *probably,* confused Jason sitting on his own. It's not like she was given the chance to be made aware if Jason's intentions were romantic or just friendly—even if she wanted the latter to be true.

"What the fuck is wrong with you?" she snapped, harshly stopping in her tracks as she jabbed her finger at him.

"I don't know what you're talking about." He shrugged his shoulders.

"She snores? She takes up the space? As if it already wasn't bad enough living with a pain, are you trying to make me sound as if I slept with you?" she replied angrily.

"What's the problem?" Zack said. "I was doing you a favour by getting rid of the guy."

"No, you weren't doing me a favour."

"I was."

"No, you weren't."

"I was."

"No."

"Yes."

"No."

"Yes."

"Ah!" she snapped, throwing her hands in the air and trying her best to subtly contain her anger. "Will you quit it? How old are you? Ten? Why is it our conversations can go from a high to ultimate off the scales annoying? I preferred it when you were bloody nagging over some project this morning than this." She shook her head. "Just because I need you for rent doesn't mean I have to like you."

"Now, I think that's a lie. A kiss isn't just a kiss, *darling*," he said.

CHAPTER SEVEN

ZACK

So he had snooped about. Turned out Project 34 had been deliberately *fiddled* with. His information didn't correspond to what he read downstairs. And there was just no way an accountant could mess up math. *No way.*

Zack sighed as he slouched back in his chair. He looked at his watch. He had about ten minutes until Claire would be howling his name, wondering where the bloody hell he'd run off to.

His phone began to ring.

"Hello, *Kyle*," he answered as he slid the caller button. "What do you want?"

"I'm just checking in, that's all. Can a friend not be concerned with his friend's interests?" Kyle replied sarcastically.

"How sweet of you," Zack said, spinning his chair side to side gently.

"So, how is it going?" he hinted.

"Well, it's only been three days, pal. I'd hardly

call it a challenge at the moment. Besides, I'm more concerned that someone has deliberately sabotaged a datasheet for that renewable trial I had tested. Not that it would grasp your attention, would it? But you asked." Zack rolled his eyes. He soon looked at the computer screen, acknowledging the flashing notification begging for his attention.

It would have been a lot more obvious to somebody else as he mumbled yes over and over, ignoring Kyle as he clicked on the email.

Three months' planning.

He read it before repeating it aloud.

"Three months what?" Kyle mimicked.

"Nothi—I mean, I could do this for three months, couldn't I?" he said.

"What do you mean?"

"Look, if I do this for three months, I could ensure the planning for this project doesn't get sabotaged at the same time. I suspect it's someone in the sales and marketing department. And that way I can also ensure enough effort is put into this for it to be successful this time, right?" he clarified as he tapped the end of his pencil upon the desk.

"I have no—"

"Three months *at least,* anyway. And it gives me enough time to understand whatever stupid moral message you're trying to get across."

"Okay, I mean, I was just gonna say for another two weeks. But three months? You're taking a gamble, *for sure.* Hey, look, I can tell you're readying to go, so I was just phoning to see if you wanted to come out Saturday. Just because you're supposed to be living normally doesn't mean you can't enjoy a good drink. So, you gonna come?" Kyle asked.

Zack was hesitant to answer.

"No strings attached. This isn't me trying to fool you. Saturday drink. That's all."

"Fine."

"See you then."

Zack hung up.

Three months? He could handle that, couldn't he? But he had to, especially if he was suspicious that something wasn't entirely playing out right within that department. No wonder he'd lost support from the board and his father branded it as stupid. But never mind that; he had the chance to change that this time around. He just had to make sure everything worked out smoothly. First, announce the plans and ensure planning permission was *mission-go* from the council he had to visit sometime this week, and then build, secure, and profit. It seemed a legitimate plan. *Right?*

***

CLAIRE

She was struggling to concentrate on the figures ahead as her nagging conscience wondered where on earth Zack had been for the last twenty minutes or so. No man needed to use the toilet for that long unless he came in contact with some bad takeaway. Although he could be hiding, considering she was threatening to castrate him for embarrassing her in front of Jason like that earlier on. Or there was option three: Monica. Let's be honest, she'd suspected it from day one when she'd seen the pair glued next to each other. Not that she would be jealous or anything. *Pssf.* A kiss was just a kiss. A mere mistake. A foolish frustration that probably proved Darren's theory of her being very sexually frustrated. *No, definitely not that.*

Claire's ears perked up when she heard a high-pitched giggle sprout from Darren's direction. Interested, she stood up, leaning over the cubicle to have a look.

"No, you hang up first." A low purr penetrated through the chambers of his throat. She arched her brow up, stepping back down before sweeping out of her cubicle and into his.

"And who was that?" she interrogated, her suspicions growing from the smile growing on his lips.

"No one," he softly said, batting his eyelashes as he placed his phone down onto a padded notebook set before him.

"Darren," she insisted, "I think I have the right considering you left me at lunch. Now, tell, tell." She knew those red blushing cheeks weren't admitting guilt but were meant to show something else.

"Ah, dang it!" he exhaled. "You win. I didn't want to tell you yet just in case things weren't definite. But...fine." He sounded defeated but not vexed to share as he ushered her in closer. "So, you know that next door neighbour I've mentioned?"

"Yeah?"

"Well, I could say we've met for a coffee date,

and I could say we're moving pretty fast," he suggested, his cheeks reddening even more as he struggled not to squirm on the spot.

"What, really?" she buzzed.

"Yes! Oh, Claire!" he whispered excitedly. "We bumped into each other for real the other day. He'd locked himself out his apartment, so I invited him in, and well, we just hit it off. He's such a darling. Honestly, I didn't care if he was gay, but he was so affectionate, flirtatious, and all that jazz," he explained, and for a split second, he appeared as if his daydreams had swooped him up.

"Oh, Darren. I'm so glad," Claire said earnestly, giving him a brief side hug. "And? Did anything happen?"

"We did kiss. He sort of did that cliché there's-an-eyelash-under-your-eye before moving in to kiss me. The locksmith came all too soon before things escalated, but I'm glad, because I didn't just want it to be all about sex. We had been speaking for ages, and I liked his character. Anyway, he gave me his number, and we went for lunch last weekend. I'm sorry I never told you about that, but I didn't want to tell anyone until I was a hundred percent sure things weren't going to be a flop. You know? He'd just sleep with me then ignore me. I genuinely like him, though, and we've both agreed to take things slow. You forgive me, though?" he said, defensively covering his face with his hand.

"Oh, shut up. Of course I do. Why would I be mad?" She chuckled. "I'm more than happy for you, Darren. That's all that matters to me."

"Thank God, babes," he sighed with relief. "I

really did not want to be in your bad books. Anyway, I suspect you shall soon reveal that you did indeed sleep with Mr. Handsome-Socks. All in good time."

"Oh, ha ha." *Although she had kissed Zack, so there was some truth in that sense.*

It shouldn't have come as a surprise, nor should it have vexed her when she witnessed Monica curling under Zack's arm as she playfully tapped the end of his nose near the lifts. Why should she care? She tried to ignore it as she turned her attention to Darren's work and blatantly attempted to appear interested and helpful as he answered her few questions.

"Sorry," Zack said at her desk.

She turned to face him, begging herself to not appear bothered or aware of Zack's antics.

"Just let's get back to work," she said, ignoring that she was ticked off that she'd seen him with Monica for the second time now.

***

ZACK

Bad move. He should have thought twice. It wasn't exactly smart, but it had been done now. Any idiot could see he'd hooked up with Monica, perhaps, not where, but they could see he had been intoxicated in lust for several minutes, fucking her roughly against a wall. It wasn't meant to happen, but it did. He liked to think it was bound to happen with the several condoms stashed behind the chunk of credit cards in his wallet.

Claire still hadn't breathed a word. She was too busy typing away on the keyboard, looking as if she hadn't given a thought to where he had been for the last thirty minutes or so.

At half four, another half hour before clock out, Graves made an announcement just as Zack suspected he would. It didn't make sense to bore through the details, but essentially it made the department clear that there was another project that the CEO wanted them to focus on instead. It was announced as Project 42. It would be the construction of a housing district, *all renewable homes*.

"Wow," Claire said beside him. "Another one. Let's hope this doesn't turn out to be another disaster."

"I'm sure it won't," he remarked, inwardly hoping there was a pinch of truth to what he said.

Claire was already shuffling her things together, collecting her pencil case and odd slips of paper as she shoved them into her handbag. He watched with interest as she took out her purse and inspected inside. It was near enough five now, and most of the other colleagues were heading out in small packs.

"Just so you know, my way of showing some hospitality has expired. And I'm guessing your side of the shelves in the kitchen are *still* empty. I'm going food shopping now, so if you want to tag along, you're welcome to," she said, her interest still glued to the inside of her purse.

Zack swallowed. "Shopping?"

"Yes."

"Don't you order it in or—"

"If I was able to afford a maid or continually afford to get shopping home delivered, I would, but these days, nothing is cheap or free," she interjected, sliding her purse back into her bag. Claire ran her fingers through her hair as she pushed back the loose strands from out of her face. "I'm starting to suspect that you've come from a privileged background," she added, leaning forward to switch off the computer monitor.

"*Ha ha,* you could say that." He chuckled anxiously as he scratched the back of his head.

***

CLAIRE

"Okay, let's see," she muttered, scanning the contents within the caged trolley. "Wait." She held her hand out to stop Zack. "Does this look like what I asked for?"

Zack shrugged his shoulders. "I followed what you said," he lied, knowing for a fact he rushed towards the aisle and grabbed the nearest packet just so he wouldn't have to endure this crammed-up space any longer. How on earth people managed, he didn't have a clue. It was like a stampede around here; the yellowish, pale floor was thick already with footprints and black indented marks from trolley wheels constantly tearing up its track.

"Since when do the four packets of hula-hoops I asked for look like French fries?" she sighed, grasping them out of the trolley.

"They're the same, pretty much, aren't they?"

Claire blinked. "Excuse me? No, no, no. Hula-hoops are *not* the same as French Fries. Are you out of your mind?"

"They're just a packet of crisps," he replied, shrugging his shoulders once again.

"You're actually crazy," she said, shaking her head. "Actually *crazy*. Remind me to never split the bill with you again. You're on your own next time. I take this as a personal insult." She began lightly steering the trolley to the right as he followed her down the aisle and then into another.

They headed back into the aisle he had hastily entered just moments before. She took no more time as she shoved the packet back into its original position and selected the packet on the shelf above.

"See? Now, that wasn't effort, was it?" She rolled her eyes as she placed it into the trolley.

"Oh, I *deeply* apologise," he joked.

"Idiot," she hissed.

Beside her, she heard someone chuckle lightly. Claire hadn't noticed her at first, but this elderly woman dressed from head to toe in bright florals was confident and friendly enough to intrude, placing a hand on Claire's arm briefly. "Oh, you two remind me of my husband when we'd ramble on. Newlyweds?" she asked, a harmless smile on her face as two blue eyes inquisitively looked at her own.

"Ah, ha ha, no—"

"It's been a year, hasn't it, love?" Zack interrupted, intruding Claire's personal space as he draped his arm loosely around her shoulder.

"Oh, that's lovely," the elderly woman replied, her eyes melting with happiness. "I'll tell you, it will only get better. Trust me, I'm the expert."

Claire couldn't deprive an old woman's happiness, so she smiled through her teeth. As soon as the woman had moved out of earshot, Claire turned on her heel and stamped on his right shoe.

"Son-of-a-frog! What have you got in your shoes, a house brick?" he grumbled as he bent down to console his foot.

"You're lucky I hadn't," she warned. "No way would I ever marry you." She watched as he composed himself and stood back up after attempting to rub his fingers across the top of his smart, black shoe.

"Ouch. I thought we would have made a lovely couple. We've got the sexual tension already," he said, a slight grin on his lips.

"And that's where you can fuck off."

CHAPTER EIGHT

ZACK

Just because he couldn't treat himself to lavish meals, it didn't mean he would allow himself to slack on exercise. He'd joined one of the local gyms, which left him about two hundred quid in his pocket after paying yesterday's rent and splitting the bill halfway on shopping. It was rather strange limiting himself to eight hundred every month, but it was just for three months until he was sure the project would be successfully accepted through the board. He couldn't remember the last time he'd been restricted, money-wise. His allowance as a kid was a maximum of £15,000 but was controlled and regulated, so there was that time.

Beads of sweat lingered on his brow as he jabbed a couple of punches to the red punching bag hooked up from the ceiling. A gym was a gym, so he needed not complain, considering the atmosphere was the same in the upscale one he'd used to attend every week up until now. It was barely six, but he couldn't sleep. Olivia had emailed him last night notifying him that the local council wanted a meeting in relation to the plot of land he'd secured until construction could begin.

At around half eight, he'd asked Olivia to electronically clock him in—so at least his false identity wouldn't get red flagged for absence—and accepted that he would have to rely on Wickes, his personal driver and a close family friend, Kyle's father in fact, to chauffeur him to the meeting.

If there was anything he'd desperately missed, it was the sight of a Rolls Royce rolling up to the curb, glistening and edgy. His heart panged with relief. Zack expressed his gratitude as Wickes got out the driver's side and smoothly opened the backdoor for him.

"It's good to see you, Wickes," Zack confessed, literally bouncing inside with bubbles of excitement.

"As ever good to see you, Mr. Benson," he replied as he got into the driver's seat and took the car out of neutral.

"I presume you received my message from my PA?" Zack asked, looking to the rear mirror.

"Yes, she informed me you'd be vacant here and there," he answered politely, his attention glued to the road as they turned off into a right corner.

Wickes had been part of the family since his father's remaining years as CEO before he positioned Zack to take over the business. He was a reliable, honest, and loyal man whom served in the Royal Air Force during his younger years and was awarded for his bravery for protecting a VIP. After that, he'd retired and secluded himself in the countryside, married to his childhood sweetheart and their two children. Unfortunately, things did not go as planned, and sadly Wickes lost his wife in a car accident on the narrow country lanes, leaving him to protect his two children, the only family he had left. Zack's father, Elijah Benson, met Wickes during his visit to the Lake District; their encounter couldn't have been more eventful. Wickes had saved his father's life pushing him away from an oncoming car heading for them both; thankfully, they both made it without a scratch. Since that day, Wickes had been part of the family and his two kids, close in age to Zack and Jared, became the closest of friends. Therefore, it wasn't surprising that Kyle was Zack's best friend. Truth was he could get angry with Kyle, could despise his guts at times, but that couldn't change how much he admired his spirit.

It must have been twenty minutes before they arrived at their destination. It wasn't that hard to miss with the derelict land and the crowd of yellow helmets and green visibility jackets safeguarding the site in the centre. The land itself was just a mile out of town, a neighbouring community of spread out, mixed-terraced and semi-detached houses, mostly council owned. The land itself used to hold a factory. To put it into proportion, the land was large enough for an entire football stadium.

Wickes followed Zack as they took a jacket and helmet each before venturing across the rocky terrain towards the group of council officials. He hadn't needed to introduce himself, nor did he expect to when he acknowledged a slender, tallish woman with bright purple curly hair. She extended her hand out towards him.

"Good morning, Mr Benson, I'm Sandra. I believe we've spoken on the phone several times," she introduced herself. She smiled, oblivious that her red lipstick had stained the front of her teeth.

"Yes, so, I believe this is just a necessary call to grab details and what not?" he asked, suspicious that her friendly smile deflated little by little. "I'm correct, aren't I? Everything will remain approved?"

"*Actually,* I'm afraid we're unable to secure this plot of land for you any longer. It appears that local residents aren't too keen on the local investment, and we've received alternative options that would appear more suitable. Of course, this isn't official yet, and you still have the chance to keep this land, but I'd strongly advise that you reconsider, as residents can form petitions, which would only waste your time and money. We can offer you compensation for the fee already paid to secure the land," she explained, her smile forced now as she gripped the black clipboard tightly.

"What?" He frowned. "This is obscene. You said we had approval from the council since day one, especially considering that we're a private investment. That should be more than enough. And I thought this was confidential towards planning. How on earth have you secured other competitors looking to buy this land?" He was beyond disbelief. He was hoping this was a bad nightmare and he'd wake up.

She fiddled briefly with her shirt collar. "Mr. Benson, I can only apologise. The council has been pitched on a new shopping centre, which we've sampled towards residents, and they agree they'd prefer that to your option."

"*Really?* A shopping centre? Isn't there bloody enough of them? Do you not understand the effort I've implemented to ensure that this project goes forth? I don't want to hear what you *advise*," he said bitterly, "or that I should *reconsider* my options, because I have already decided that this area would be beneficial for my project. It would also benefit yourselves, what with the housing crisis and threat of global warming." He was feeling tenser, and that wasn't because of this morning.

"Mr. Benson, I apologise, but that is that. We haven't officially decided, so your chances of maintaining this land, although slim, can be secured. You just have to be willing to present your project to the council and prominent members of the local community. If so, I'll email you the details if you decide not to withdraw," she said, straightening up a little before bidding him goodbye as she turned towards the people congregated in the centre of the field.

He was about to kick off until some fairly pudgy woman scooted on over, soliciting his attention. "Mr. Benson?" She held out a hand. He was hesitant to shake it and rightly so when she introduced her business. "I'm Kelly Brookstones. I work for Label Works. Unfortunately, the project manager couldn't make it today, but he sent me out to discuss plans about this site. I presume you're aware we're the UK's leading corporation in the shopping industry, and of course, we have plans to construct here. I'd strongly advise it would be best if you consider withdrawing. We'd be happy to take this off your hands," she said, a sinister smile jumping out at him.

Zack frowned with a dry, short laugh. "Oh, so you're the competitors. I don't think I'm exactly convinced to *reconsider* my options. Do I look convinced?" His frown stretched as he arched his right brow.

"Mr. Benson—"

"*Kelly.*"

"You'll be doing yourself a favour if you withdraw," she said, proudly stiffening up.

"I don't think I'm willing to do so. I guess we shall be seeing each other soon," he replied, daggering his eyes at Sandra, the council official who returned, probably hoping Kelly's sweet talk had done the deal. "I'll expect you to contact me," he instructed to Sandra before turning and heading away alongside Wickes.

"Absolute bullshit," he muttered to himself.

***

CLAIRE

Don't say it. Why are you thinking it? Stop. Where was Zack? *Okay, she said it.* It's done.

But for real, she was a little concerned. *No.* Not concerned. *Interested?* No. How could she make it sound like she wasn't bothered, while she was wondering where on earth he was? *How about let's just give no thought to it?* After all, she should have been bitter, considering Graves had plopped another file onto her desk asking her to trim and tidy it up. And who's work should it be? *Monica's.*

Darren was holding a cup of tea as he came on over. "Bloody hell, how many files you got on that desk? All product datasheets?" he stated, leaning on the inside wall of her cubicle.

Claire sighed. "Blame Graves. He keeps piling Monica's work on my desk. Whether it's intentional or not, I don't think that's a good sign for giving her the promotion."

"Damn, babes. You should report that or tell him straight to his face," he suggested, shaking his head as he prodded his finger into his cup of tea. "Ouch, it's a bit hot."

"I'm thinking of telling him because this is getting ridiculous, but then I'm also hoping he might change his mind if he sees that I'm completing the work," she claimed, propping her elbow onto the desk and leaning her head into the palm of her hand.

"Or he might just continue to do so and pass your work off as Monica's," he objected, kissing his teeth. "Oh, yeah, I have another date this Saturday. Just like yours and Jason's. How cute."

"We're not going on a date." She rolled her eyes.

"Yeah, whatever you say."

Darren scooted around to his cubicle just as a great force of energy rocketed past her, then sat down, abusing the chair beside her, and threw his phone, apartment keys, and wallet onto the desk, missing the computer monitor by inches. Her face was a look of concern as she asked if he were okay.

"What's got your pants in a twist?" she remarked, hoping humour would fix his attitude.

"Not now, I can't handle *your* crap," he snapped. Zack sighed, running his hand through his hair, not aware at first that his bitterness had offended her.

"Oh, *sorry.* I'm sorry I was trying to show some concern. *Fuck you,* then," she hissed, turning in her chair and trying to resume whatever was on the screen. It turned out to be just a blank, open Word document.

"Ah, I didn't mean it—"

"I don't want to hear it. Just do the task I've assigned," she interrupted rudely.

***

ZACK

Zack felt incredibly bad. It wasn't his intention to upset or offend her. He was just peed off about the council and that land he'd *secured* for constructing renewable homes. Zack was still trying to wrap his mind around it all. Someone had breached the contract; there wasn't supposed to be any mention of the land being renovated. How on earth Label Works found out, he didn't know. And now, his anger had annoyed someone else. *There is just no winning, is there?*

"Claire," he meekly said but soon shut up.

He decided it was best to leave her be.

At around one o'clock, as Zack expected, Graves

announced to the department that Project 42 was pending.

"As of this morning, all departments have been notified that Project 42 will remain pending. Instead, we've been asked to produce a team in support with other leading department teams to essentially speed up on planning and form one that will be presentable to the council and leading members of the community as plans have suddenly been altered due to a competitor," he explained, fresh sweat glimmering on his forehead from under the ceiling light above, and there was the sight of sweat patches every time he lifted his arms up. "Please remain aware that I'll personally be selecting a team today who are required to stay overtime to receive instructions. Thank you."

"Claire?"

Still as stubborn as a mule.

***

CLAIRE

She couldn't find the will to answer him. She was deeply offended. As much as she liked to say she despised the guy, a lot had happened in four days. They'd kissed, rambled on, and were developing a sort of love/hate relationship. But there was no way she'd fall for him, like that book she'd once read that told the story of two lovers falling for one another after hating each other at first sight. *No way.* This wasn't going to be no cheesy romance. This was real life.

After a while, she relaxed a bit and was about to approach him when an email notification swooped onto her screen. "Great," she grumbled, leaning back in her chair. Turned out she had been chosen as one of the lucky few who would be participating with this mission to getting Project 42 back on track. So was Zack.

"What?" he dared to ask.

She exhaled. "We're both on project duties."

He didn't seem to be fussed when she glanced over.

"Oh."

And *oh* was just how she felt when five o'clock came around, and she, Zack, and three more stood outside Graves' office as if they were waiting to see the headmaster. Graves soon came out, wearing a blue dotted white shirt, sweating a little in places, and his grey hair combed back.

"Come on in," he said.

Everyone slipped in. She took the far corner nearest the pale green wall that looked like it was stuck in the eighties, including the cliché plotted plant that desperately needed water. Graves took the lead, standing in front of his desk, backed by the giant window looking out to neighbouring skyscrapers and the darkening sky.

"Again, congratulations on being the select few who have made it through. I'll try not to keep you long, because I expect to go through this in more detail tomorrow, but for now, I'm going to make it *very* clear that Mr. Benson expects a high amount of effort. This is important towards Project 42's progress," he explained, demonstrating with the use of his hands the severity of the situation.

"So." He paused, glancing around at every single face. "There's five of us. So, Claire, I'm partnering you up with Zack, considering you're mentoring him anyway. The rest of you, team up. Unfortunately, there's no dropping out of this. I've chosen you lot for a reason. So tomorrow morning, nine a.m. sharp. You're free to leave."

Several members of the group headed through the door, leaving Claire and Zack last. She was leaving too until Graves called her back.

"*Claire,* I want to thank you for chasing up on Monica's work. Again, I apologise that you didn't get the promotion, but it was a sharp competition between you two. You understand, *right*?" His tone was beyond patronizing.

"*Actually—*"

"Okay, good talk." He smiled, ushering her out of the door. It slammed behind her.

"Everything okay?" Zack asked.

"No, but I can't do shit about it," she confessed aloud.

"Look, I'm sorry about earlier. I had a shitty morning, but that gave me no excuse to talk to you the way I did," he apologised.

"I *suppose* I can forgive you," she teased, grabbing her bag off her desk.

"Good, because I really don't want to be castrated, thank you very much," he remarked, running his hand across his jaw.

"Too bad. I left my garden clippers at home," she joked, smiling to herself, her back thankfully facing him. She preferred the ambiguity of her body language; she'd rather he didn't see her face.

It was exhausting being stubborn, so it was probably why she let it slide and forgave him. He should have considered himself lucky because her stubbornness could stretch on for days if she wanted. Claire liked to think she held a world record for it. And that was saying something.

The pair headed out of the building, Zack close behind, looking critically at his phone while Claire led the way towards the bus stop. She was thankful she hadn't needed an umbrella when she looked at the forecast because there was no way her flimsy cargo jacket could fight against rain.

"So what did he *exactly* say to you in there?" Zack prodded, his phone tucked away in his trouser pocket now.

Claire exhaled, tucking her hands into her pockets. "It was about the promotion I didn't get. And *thanking* me for doing Monica's work," she replied earnestly, accepting that this was just the way things were.

"Shit," he cursed, scratching the end of his nose, suddenly bashful on the subject. Although, if Claire recalled, she had seen the pair walking side by side earlier. Possibly, something did occur. *Not like she cared. Psssf.* It wasn't her problem. Just problematic doing Monica's work, that was all.

"Yeah, *well*, that's life. Until Graves leaves, that's what we're stuck with. A male whore," she grumbled, defeatedly looking at the pointy end of her heels. "I think that about summarizes him. I do care about not getting the promotion, but I wouldn't have minded if I didn't have to do *her* work. It's stupid." She looked up and acknowledged the scrutiny painted across his face as he stared off into the road. "And now, we've got this project, which means I'll have to catch up with my work. It's not like the *top dog* is aware of that. I got last month's datasheet to do yet before I can send it to accounting. And I've got tons of customer sample questionnaires, and our clients, and our shareholders—bloody tons of work! Gee, I honestly don't know how I cope with stress these days."

Zack remained quiet, not breathing a word. She was kind of hoping for a response, perhaps a shared understanding, but then she remembered he'd just started on the job, and like she was beginning to suspect, he hadn't had to handle this sort of stress yet. Claire had kind of manipulated a back story for him—he was a privileged boy, probably middle class, never worked a day through University and just got into his first job. *Maybe that was a bit harsh.*

"So," she piped up, leaning herself against the tall wall that circled around as part of the accessible, disabled walkway. "Look, I'm not judging...or *maybe* I am." She paused, licking her tongue against the roof of her mouth. "But are you sure this is the kind of work you want to do? I mean, you don't look—I mean, you look like you should be in modelling or some other business. And no, that is no reflection on my opinion towards you. That *incident* didn't mean a thing." She cleared her throat, irritated at the vivid images flunking her mind.

116

*** *

ZACK

Zack chuckled, a daring smile broadening across his lips. "No, it's okay, you can't help the way you feel," he said, pausing momentarily as she rolled her eyes. "I mean, they say never judge a book by its cover, right? I guess...I wasn't cut out for all that razzle dazzle, even if I look like I could be on the front of a Gucci product," he joked, then he paused for a few seconds. "I have a confession to make." He smiled, leaning his right arm on the wall to face her.

"What?"

"I used to own a small business, *technically*," he lied. "But it went wrong. So I left it."

"What happened?" she asked.

He kissed the front of his teeth, rolling his head to the left side. "I wasn't allowed to express my creativity. You see, although I owned the business, I didn't. You get me? *No*?" he hinted, continuing to explain as she shook her head. "Well, there was someone above, like there always is. He didn't like the direction I was taking the company, so, *well,* we could never agree. So I left. Money ran out eventually, so I couldn't buy him out. He was really a partner, if you want to put it like that. I needed a job, so here I am." He tried his best to appear convincing despite the smile he held.

It was kind of funny, to think of it. Zack lied, but it wasn't all *lie*. His father deeply disapproved. He didn't want his son to channel renewability into the scheme of things. But Zack wouldn't run out of money, nor could he really leave unless his father or the board, whom he suspected were tight together, hired someone else. Not that it would look good on his father's behalf, hiring someone who wasn't a blood relative.

"Oh." She slowly nodded, standing up from off the wall as the bus pulled up to the curb.

"Does that answer your questions?" he sneered, sitting down beside her on the patchy, green-clothed seats. She appeared convinced by the expression on her face, but that didn't mean she was completely satisfied.

Claire rolled her eyes, smiling just a little. "Oh, of *course*."

"And my stuff? I don't really like materialistic things."

Claire snorted. "So, what, you don't call a bed or wardrobe or anything else for that matter important?"

"Oh, yeah, but your apartment was already well equipped. So I needn't bother," he said.

***

At around seven, they'd managed to break free from the waves of traffic and returned safely to the apartment. Claire held a self-satisfied smile; it was like a trophy she could wave about as she humourlessly watched Zack attempt to chop up carrots. That was another thing he had to soon confess: he barely knew how to cook. It was also *his* turn to cook.

"I honestly can't do this," he moaned, dropping the knife on the side of the chopping board.

"Yes, you can," she insisted. "Literally, you've managed two slices. You can do the rest. It's not rocket science."

"I could *seriously* chop off my finger," he argued. This situation was an entire insult to his *masculinity*.

"No...no, you can't. Not if you just take your time. How on earth you've managed to survive all these years, I'll never know. Just, here," she said, taking the knife and ushering him aside. "Watch." Then she began slowly chopping the remaining carrot. "See? Easy."

"Nope." He shook his head. "I refuse."

She dropped the knife and planted her hand onto her hip. "And so you're just gonna live off take-away menus? Because I am certainly not cooking for you. If you want to have the same meals, you've got to contribute. If not, you're on your own, buster," she said.

Zack sighed, playing with the edge of his white shirt. It was like a magnet, because where else did her eyes dart next? "I'm sorry," he gleefully replied. "It's a little hot in here, don't you think?" He watched as she awkwardly looked away, swallowing hard.

"I know what you're trying to do, and it's not going to work," she remarked.

"I mean..." He continued waving his top about. "It's so hot right now. I think I need to take my top off," he teased.

"Don't you da—"

With a swift move, he took it off. What else could her eyes do but praise his layers and layers of muscles? She immediately scoffed, looking away.

"Ah, much better," he hollered, pumping his arms forward and back that impressively flaunted his toned, masculine physique.

Claire frowned. "Idiot."

"What was that? I couldn't hear you." Zack cupped his hand to his ear. "I'll come closer." When he stepped forward, Claire jogged back a couple.

"No, no!" she squealed as he chased her around the kitchen.

Zack soon grabbed her tight, laughing as she squealed helplessly. She certainly wasn't complaining at the two broad, bear-like arms snaking around her.

"I swear—you—are so infuriating," she said, struggling to fight free.

She was still laughing even as he let her go.

"Oh God," he exhaled, a little out of breath. "I think this calls for a take-away, don't you?"

Chapter Nine

ZACK

Saturday came.

And it also brought along with it another pile of work. Project 42. Yesterday brought the schemes of things together. They simply had to convince the council that people wanted their concept. Even if Zack hadn't been assigned to the task with Claire, he would have nosed in somehow, considering this was significant towards the development. And if there was, let's just say a traitor, someone fiddling with data, it'd be the perfect time to catch them out.

They'd been planning it all yesterday and some this morning. Now, he had just gotten out of the shower, wiping the soap suds from out of his ears with a small hand towel as he crept towards Claire, who was still working hard at it. He glanced over her shoulder, watching her detail their shared information by presenting it as a mind-map for reference before they'd work together to type it up neatly as a PowerPoint presentation.

"So, are you doing anything today?" he asked, leaning his hand on the back of her kitchen chair.

She put down her pen. "Nope. I'm gonna finish up our notes, then I need to look over last year's datasheets. I don't suppose you're gonna do that?"

He gave a short laugh. "I have plans, so *no*. But I'll look over this later." He mockingly saluted as he dropped the towel on the table. "As a matter of fact, I'm off now, so *farewell*, m'lady."

"Thank God! I can finally have peace around here," she said as he began to walk off.

***

As promised, he showed up at his penthouse, as if he needed to be invited. His brother, Jared, and friend, Kyle, were polishing off the last drop of alcohol from his drinks cabinet. He expected this. But what he didn't expect was his mother welcoming him from the other side of the room, cradling a grey designer's bag that he preferred over the pout clinging to her pink lips.

"Zack *Harold* Benson," she said, her white pearl dangling earrings shimmering aggressively as she stalked towards him. "I've left tons of messages on that answer machine of yours. I come to visit and arrive to see Jared passed out on the sofa and Kyle parading about in his underwear. I had the shock of my life!" *Great,* he thought. He narrowed his eyes at the pair, who were bashfully tidying up their mess, glasses nearly being knocked over in the process.

"Mother, I apologise—"

"Where were you?" she asked, grabbing a tissue from out of her bag and dabbing herself under her nose.

"I was at the office," he lied.

"Well, *next time,* answer your home phone, and for goodness' sake, Zack, control your brother. He's yet to be a proper adult. I don't want to see him passed out," she demanded, pausing as she exhaled. "Now, I came to tell you that your father would like to speak to you tomorrow. It's important." She adjusted the sleeve of her navy blue jacket as she balanced her bag strap across her arm.

"Let me guess. It has to relate with that recent charity gala—and oh, yeah! Another warning or so, or to remind me not to consider renewability as an option for the company to take," he responded, sighing as he passed his mother and headed towards the drinks cabinet himself. Zack could hear his mother behind him, pestering Jared briefly, who was complaining of feeling nauseated. He poured himself a whiskey, what was left of the stuff, anyway.

"Zack, I know it's hard to hear, but your father is right. He just wants what is best for the company, for you, for all of us. It'd be embarrassing if things went wrong, and you know it would."

"And? At least I tried. I don't see the problem. I'm not scrapping our original product. Housing remains housing. I just want to experiment, work in a field that I see will be investable." He took a sip.

She exhaled. "Why you can't just follow simple instructions? You never have been able to. Just promise me you'll come tomorrow."

Zack hesitated, then nodded.

"Good, now clear this place up. You're not in University anymore. You're a grown man." She kissed his cheek, leaving remnants of her lipstick upon his right cheek. "Jared, fix yourself," she ordered before composing herself as she confidently walked towards the penthouse lift.

"Nice going, dickhead," Zack remarked as Kyle headed towards the opposite side of the cabinet. "What do you call this?" He gestured towards the mess of empty bottles and cans lying about.

"Man, I didn't know your mother was coming. I just forgot where I put my trousers, that was all. Your brother was high on life. What can I say?" He shrugged his shoulders.

"You have your own apartment."

"Yeah, but yours is better, and besides," Kyle argued, gently slapping Zack's shoulder, "your place is a lot nearer. Distance wouldn't have persuaded those two lovely female companions to dally on back with me and Jared. And you wouldn't have wanted poor ol' me and Jared rejected, now, would you? So, cheer up." He placed a glass down, gesturing for Zack to fill him up. "Anyway, how are things going?"

"Shit. Turns out the three months I intended to use to plan whilst doing all this funny business is in jeopardy, but I'm remaining on it now in an attempt to save the project. Not that it means anything to you, does it?" he explained. "I should honestly start thinking about changing my code to stop you pair from dropping in."

"Come, come, you wouldn't do that. Besides,

you think Jared would rather be spending his time off from his semester at the family home with two barmy parents? I think not," Kyle objected, shaking his head as he poured himself a glass of water from the kitchen sink. "So, *anyway*, I'd rather hear about interesting stuff than work. A man like me who barely likes to cooperate with that responsibility cares not to think about that. What's the situation with the roommate? Any valuable lessons being learned? Can she not keep her hands off *you?*"

"Actually, she's *very* stubborn. And I've not been that entirely invested in trying to sleep with her, if that's what you're implying. We do have sexual tension, *though*. And *she* knows it," Zack said, swirling the dark liquid around in the glass. "And one could say I've attempted…washing up." He looked towards the floor.

"I'd have paid to have seen that. Zack, washing up. Bloody hell!" He laughed. "Your mother would be having the fits!"

"She probably would," Zack agreed. "Look, I honestly don't know what you've planned today, but I actually need to dig a few things out of my office."

"Aye, aye. Well, Jared is still under the weather, so I'm gonna patch him up. You're coming out as you promised, *right?* Later? It's important you do, as it'll be the club I intend to invest into," Kyle said proudly, passing Zack's brother, who was struggling to lean up off the couch.

"Oh, wow. Looks like Kyle does have legs, arms, and *a brain*. Wonders will never cease," Zack sneered.

"Well, my business bachelor's degree had to come useful for something."

***

CLAIRE

Claire was researching through last year's figures, comparing the old Project 32 to the new, perhaps already prematurely dying Project 42. Investment would have to be increased. There was clientele there, investors were out there, and with current government legislation, using renewable sources had to be increased. She was marking it down, cross-referencing the old to the new before her mobile rang, summoning her to stop. She didn't expect it to be Jason ringing at half three, considering their meet-up was not till later, unless he was double checking as friends usually do to see if she was still available.

She picked it up, relieved to see it was her mother's face lit up on the caller ID. "Hello, Mom. What's up?" she said, leaning back in the kitchen chair.

"Oh, honey. I'm just calling to see how you are," she replied joyfully.

"Oh, yeah. I'm fine. I was gonna call you. Sorry, I've been busy. I had to sort out finding a new roommate. It's done now, so don't worry. I've paid this month's rent." Claire stood up and began to pace around the room.

"Oh, good. I'm glad to hear. Have—I mean, you're going to bring someone to Matt's wedding, right?" she asked, referring to Claire's brother, Matthew.

"Mommmm," she groaned, "it's not necessary. I don't have to bring a date. The invitations just suggest that for those who want to bring a plus one." She propped herself on top of the counter, kicking her feet gently against the lower cupboard doors.

"I know, but it'd be nice. Oh, Claire, I know it's your brother's day, but it would be nice if you could. You're so beautiful, honey. It just baffles me how you're still single," she insisted.

"Gee, thanks for reminding me, Mom. Look, I don't know yet, but don't go putting your hopes up if I don't. Just remember, it's Matt's day. Not mine, okay?" she said.

"I know, I know. Well, it would be nice, that's all I'm saying. Anyway, I better go. You know how your father gets when he can't hear the telly. I love you, sweetheart," she replied.

"Yes, love you too. Bye, Mom," she responded, ending the phone call. If there was one thing she'd preferred, it was she'd rather be lectured for behaving badly as a child than be lectured for her current single status. Darren's voice for a second then, sprang to mind, childishly singing about Jason tonight. *This wasn't a date*, she chided back. *As if that helps. Talking to yourself.*

She looked at the clock then quickly texted Jason, asking him what time he expected to arrive. She sent him the address and any other necessary details. He surprisingly texted immediately after, supplying her the detail that he'd be there around five, the movie he'd planned was at half-five, tickets were already booked, and then they would rendezvous at a restaurant. *His exact words.*

It was four already, meaning she had an hour to get her ass kicked into action. Like military order, she wanted her legs shaved, hair washed, makeup applied, and clothed with at least five minutes to spare. *That was fair,* wasn't it? She could manage that, *right?*

***

ZACK

After, rummaging through hours of half-empty folders, he'd found nothing to indicate that his father had cooperated with some member in the workforce to mess about with Project 32's investment. There was no slip-up, but what did he expect? His father to have just gladly provided the evidence of ordering some fool to authorise it? He'd also spent much of his day caring for Jared, who was nauseated till about half past two, when he'd finally vomited up the last chunks of last night's vodka. If it was anyone, it had to be Clive Graves, the department manager. He had final judgment of the summary before being passed to the accountants. It made sense. He just needed evidence. Evidence that his father was still messing about. And as for this recent cock-up, Project 42 had to work.

He decided it was best to head back to Claire's apartment and return later to the two imbeciles after following up with Claire's progress on their project.

Zack felt tired as he got off the bus and a little dehydrated after trying not to suffocate on the awful stench coming from the elderly man sitting at the front, digging his fingers into a loaf of bread and gnawing the crusts off. He entered the apartment about quarter to five, throwing the keys onto the sideboard nearest the front door and flinging his shoes off, desperately wanting to rub his sore, aching feet.

Claire wasn't about yet. The bathroom door was wide open, and the kitchen had no wandering soul rummaging through the cupboards or boiling water in the kettle.

"Hello? Anybody home?" he called out, waiting a few seconds before flopping himself down onto the two-seater sofa. It was then a struggle and a half to reach for the remote control, surfing through the crappy late evening programmes hoping something good was on. He barely made time for television in reality. There was just no need: he was always either out, working, and setting Olivia goals she fed back to him or tousling in another stranger's bed.

"Oh, you're back. Where have you been all day?" He heard her voice grow louder as she came out of the small corridor. He was lying on his back, arm propped over his head as he peeked through the gap, almost immediately regretting his decision to have been so lazily lounging about as he collapsed onto the floor at the very sight of her. That was very *un-Zack* of him.

Speechless was an understatement. She wasn't naked, she wasn't dazzled up in a shiny, golden dress for the Oscars or some other glitzy event, but she did look stunning. For whatever reason, he didn't ask. His eyes did the asking, asking why: why did his mouth go dry at legs that looked like they went on for days? Why did his heart thump a little quicker at the little black dress hugging her curvy physique? Why was he gaping like a fish at a woman he'd spent at least a week with and now was craving her in the bedsheets he'd claimed as his? He had confessed at first sight he hadn't seen her as stunningly attractive as the models he'd swept off their feet, but now those two brown eyes indignantly looking back at his own suddenly had him tongue-tied.

"Why are you staring at me like that? It's rude, you know?" she piped up. She stood with her hands on her hips and her red lips angrily pursed together.

"You look beautiful," he confessed, halfway back up on his feet before settling back down onto the sofa.

"Oh, erm," she coughed, awkwardly dropping her hands from her hips. "Thanks, but it's really nothing. It's casual. Or I hope it is." She paused nervously.

"I mean, casual. Sure. But don't be surprised if you have a man howling at your feet," he remarked, his eyes still failing to keep at bay.

"Great. I look stupid. It's too much. Urgh. I've got to go change—"

"Baby, no, you look smoking hot," he interjected, biting down on his bottom lip and playfully fanning himself.

She rolled her eyes.

"Where are you going? You haven't got a date, have you?" he asked, interested to know where on earth this stunning beauty was heading off to. Now, he was beginning to crave her some more. If a kiss wasn't already enough, he was wanting to know what else they'd be willing to sweetly make.

***

CLAIRE

"So what if it is?" she defensively said. "I'm allowed to date."

"So you are," he persisted.

"Err...yes!" she lied, grabbing her black clutch.

"Wow...I feel kind of betrayed. You're willing to let some other guy take you out? What about poor ol' me?" he objected.

"Ha, fat chance." She stalked towards the front door, grabbing her keys from off the sideboard.

"Your zipper isn't completely up," Zack noticed.

"What? Oh?" She began to fuss over it, attempting to reach the small zip tucked nicely just below where her bra strap was. Abruptly, her heart hammered as she felt his fingertips gently touching her back. They didn't feel cold but immersed in whatever emotion she was feeling; they summoned her nerves to the surface. This sort of felt like déjà vu. Holding her breath? Her heart rate rising? Sweaty palms? And here came the intrusive thought! This sudden desire to allow him to embrace her in his arms, slowly undress her like a wrapped present before consuming each other in an animal instinct. *No.*

"Thanks." She shook off the thought as he finished zipping it up to the top.

"Are you sure you'd wouldn't rather stay here with me? I've been told I can be very entertaining," he replied, deviously smiling as he popped his hands in his trouser pockets.

Claire snorted.

It was totally unplanned then, that the door was knocked upon, abruptly simmering the tension between the pair. She opened the door. *Oh, dear.* Flowers? *Please say this wasn't a date.* Even if she had completely lied to Zack for some odd reason, admitting it as such. Claire thought she heard Zack wince as Jason greeted her affectionately, passing her the bunch of flowers and swiping a quick peck on her right cheek. *Shit.*

"You look…gorgeous." Jason blushed. "Oh." As he noticed Zack.

"Erm, thank you, Jason. You *really* didn't have to. I'll just go put them in a vase," she interjected, sliding away from the door.

Jason awkwardly pocketed his hands into his black jeans. "Hello," he managed to say.

Zack raised his brows.

"Sorry," they both heard Claire say as she returned. "I couldn't find a vase, so I just had to fill the washing bowl up with water until I go out to buy one."

"No worries." He smiled. "I'll have her back by eleven," he joked towards Zack, who appeared suddenly stung.

Then she bid goodbye to Zack as she left.

This couldn't be a date? Surely, it couldn't? This was just a friendly meet up. Friends can give each other flowers. Right? Claire was not quite sure now as she slid into the passenger side of Jason's red mini coupe, fumbling anxiously with her clutch. She would have known if Zack hadn't interrupted. And now? Who knew? And what about Zack? *Yes,* her conscience sneered. What did she just call that moments ago? It had to be something if she was actually considering sleeping with the guy. *No,* she argued back.

"I'm so glad you agreed to come out. It's good that I booked the tickets. Otherwise I'm pretty sure we wouldn't have got a seat," he said as he put the key into the ignition. "So, how was your day?"

Okay, fairly average conversation. Maybe this isn't a date after all. "Yeah, it was okay. Just catching up with a lot of work. Balancing between the two. You know how it is." She chuckled anxiously, trying to distract herself from the fact he'd slid in a CD that was notably a collection of love ballads. *Fuck. No. Maybe he just liked love ballads? Who didn't? Chill, Claire, chill.*

"Oh, unlucky. I'm up to date at the moment, so I've just been around my grandmother's helping her stack up some old stuff in the attic," he replied, tapping his fingers on the steering wheel.

"Let me feel your body under my fingertips," the duet continued from the CD. *Fuck, fuck, fuck.*

"Oh, that's so sweet of you." She forced a smile.

"Ha ha, yeah. I love helping my grandmother as much as I can. She's lovely," he replied, steering left onto the busy road, heading towards the left of the city centre where she knew the largest cinema in town stood.

"Make love till dawn breaks through." Another line in the chorus scared her. She flinched, glancing quickly outside to escape the awkwardness.

"So, erm, what are we seeing?" she asked, trying her best to keep the conversation moving.

"Action, if you don't mind. It's part of the latest superhero franchise," he proudly said.

She sighed inside with relief. "Yeah, that's fine." She smiled.

The large two-storey cinema was parked on the edge of the busy road, adjacent to several clubs, restaurants, pubs, and entertainment complexes all along the street. Jason found parking not too far from the city canal that stretched through the centre below. It soothed her nerves knowing that inside there was a crowd of people hanging around or having their tickets checked by ushers guarding the doors. Her attire wasn't out of the ordinary around here, nightlife was expected, so if anyone did question her short, black dress, they could assume she was clubbing straight after or following up with a drink.

Jason had already pre-booked, so he collected the tickets, refusing to allow Claire to pay half as she offered persistently as they headed towards the popcorn counter.

"No, no, I'm paying. I respect what you're saying, but please allow me to be chivalrous," he argued gently, passing over a twenty-pound note as he ordered a giant box of popcorn to share.

"Ah, I wish you would have let me. I just…like

being able—"

"I get it," he interrupted, "but this evening, I'm paying. I want to make this special."

Two reasons why she liked paying. One, it was the twenty-first century, she took pride in knowing she didn't expect the man to pay, but secondly, the question of whether this was a date. Although, so far, several things had already insinuated it. The CD, flowers, paying for her—what next? *The back row seats? God, have mercy on her soul.* At least say he hadn't booked the back row seats. *Please, say it was the middle row or front, anything but the back row,* she prayed as they had their tickets stamped and approved by the young usher guarding screen seven's doors.

"Ah, brilliant. We're in! I hope you don't mind, I got back row seats. They're VIP," he chirped, holding open the door for her as they intruded into the dark, black space.

Ah, shit. "Ha, yeaaah," she said, cursing inside as they followed the blue, neon LED lights crawling all the way up the aisle. *Just great. But don't get ahead of yourself, Claire,* she encouraged. *Friends can sit in the back. And like he said, VIP seats. So that couldn't mean this was a date, right?*

They'd soon sat down. Row 1, seats A and B.

Claire was trying her best to sit comfortably, opting whether she should cross her leg over or rest them in front. He must have noticed her fidgeting as he asked her several times if she was comfortable or okay and offered another several times if she wanted popcorn, which she refused each time.

Just stop, she could have screamed at herself. It

was exhausting trying to decipher the atmosphere, so she attempted to relax, scooping some sweet and salty popcorn from the box, chewing its cardboard consistency before swallowing it dry down her throat. The screen was still playing advertisements, ushers were escorting a few who couldn't find their seats, and bright, white tiny screens sprang up here and there in almost every row ahead. Jason was busy slurping on a drink, sometimes checking the time on his phone, and sometimes shuffling awkwardly. So far, nothing audacious had occurred to prove, yet again, the question of whether this was a date.

Until now. The movie must have had about half hour left. Claire, finally de-stressed and comfortable, eyes glued to the screen, was unaware that Jason was going in for the old, cliché pretend-you're-tired-arm-move. She felt it, though, when he suddenly slid his arm across her shoulders, refrained eye contact for a second before expressing an affectionate smile across his lips.

Claire could only blink.

Shit, shit, shit. Abort. Abort. What was she supposed to do? Whack him off. Shuffle her shoulder. Lean forward? She needed answers now. Oh no. He's going in for the kiss on the cheek. Quick!

Claire pretended to sneeze, leaning forward as she caught the pretend bugger within her hands. "Sorry," she whispered, acknowledging his red cheeks seen by the white flare from off the gigantic screen. "I'm just gonna pop to the loo." Then she stood up, thankful their seats were at the end, so she could escape if need be. Like *now*.

Jason must have not been too hurt or embarrassed; he was too busy obsessing over the CGI graphics as they left the cinema around eight. She could only hope he didn't see past her faux sneeze, although it was probably easier than telling him to his face that she wasn't interested.

"Did you see those effects? Definitely ten out of ten!" he said with enthusiasm.

They weren't heading back to the car; it turned out he'd booked a snazzy restaurant just a couple doors down from the cinema. They walked side by side, Jason with his hands in his pockets and Claire folding her arms, trying to keep warm in the chilly night.

"Yeah, great movie. I enjoyed it," she replied, thanking him as he held open the glass door for her. It was a lot warmer inside than out. The place was dimly lit, the front seating area had a bar and a fireplace, and amongst the edges were the rows of white-clothed tables, also booths, all lit up with small candle jars. *Great.* If this wasn't intended to be romantic, she didn't know what was.

"Hello, I have a reservation booked under the name Jason Manson," he confidently addressed the manager, who was standing behind the counter. She complied, typing for seconds on the keyboard before grabbing two menus as she escorted the pair to their designated seating area.

"Your waitress will be over in a second," she informed them before leaving them alone.

And great. Left alone.

***

ZACK

Investing into a business was something that couldn't be taken lightly. Nonetheless, at nine o'clock, Zack had watched his friend sign the contract, investing a chunk of money he'd placed on the table asking for partnership with the current manager, a chubby, bearded man wearing gold-painted rimmed shades. It had gone down in seconds, and not soon after they were chilling in the VIP balcony that looked down over the dance floor, enjoying bottles of champagne, a range of shots, and several women.

Zack hooted as he slammed the shot glass down, immediately compensated with some brunette sliding her ass down onto his lap.

"Ah, God!" he heard Kyle yell, laughing as he slapped Jared's back; Jared was coughing a little after he'd taken the vodka shot. "I feel like a million dollars. I've invested in a place I call home." He laughed some more, wrapping his arms around the blonde female who'd followed the same route as the brunette and slid rightfully onto his lap.

"Jared!" Zack shouted over the music, waving his free hand that wasn't clasped around the brunette's waist. "You've got to learn to take your drink better!" He laughed, sluggishly waving still. He was slightly drunk. Kyle joined in, slapping Jared's back some more as his friend's brother groaned, lying his head across the wet, sticky glass table.

Zack's companion purred into his ear as she boldly squeezed his junk. "How about we take this party somewhere else?"

His hardening pal couldn't argue. "I suppose I could agree with that." He stroked his fingers across her naked back.

She stood up, gently tugging his hand as she led him downstairs. Zack had little time to wave off Kyle and Jared, but he was in no condition to refuse. He'd been frustrated since this afternoon, seeing Claire dressed like that, and now, it comforted him knowing he could release that energy. Wherever they were going, she was eager to escort him along, passing through the crowds of people dancing wildly. It didn't cross his mind that they'd left the club until the chilly air hit him square in the face.

"Where are we going?" He nuzzled her neck as they stood at the curb.

"We're getting a taxi to yours." She cheekily smiled, wrapping her arms around his neck.

He must have been intoxicated because he was pretty sure as he turned his head to the right, he could see Claire halfway down the pavement exiting a building alongside Jason. Something inside stirred him to react; he let the eager brunette go, his feet leading the way as he stalked towards them.

"Hey! Where are you going!" he heard the woman yell after him.

Zack ignored her, desperately trying to catch up.

"Claire!" he called out, dismissing the few stares he received from passersby heading to the club or returning from a quiet meal.

***

CLAIRE

As if this night wasn't awkward enough already, she didn't want to believe someone was blatantly shouting out her name. She hoped someone else nearby was conveniently named Claire, but it seemed apparent as the voice got closer it was directed towards her. Jason stopped as she did, turning defensively, something she didn't mind in case this stranger happened to be a madman looking to chop a few heads off here and there.

"Zack?" she exhaled, utterly confounded by his appearance. She observed how his dark purple shirt was unbuttoned halfway, exposing flesh, his hair sticking up in a few places, and the sloppy steps he took before stopping in front of them. "What—what are you doing here? It's like—I thought you were at the apartment. Are you alone?" She sounded concerned, even proceeded to squeeze his shoulder as she checked his face.

"I'm fine." He jerked his thumb behind him lazily. "I'm out with a pal—or pals. I do have friends, just so you know," he babbled. "I just saw you."

"God, you're not drunk, are you?" she asked, feeling his forehead with the back of her right hand.

"No, pssf, I'm sober," he objected.

Jason coughed. Claire pulled back. She'd forgotten Jason was there for a second.

"Well, where are your friends? Are they—"

"Shit, no, I'll just catch a taxi back now," he interrupted, grabbing his wallet from the back pocket of his trousers.

"No. Jason, you don't mind if he tags along, do you? You're dropping me off now, anyway. Is that okay?" she asked, feeling a little cheeky, but it meant she didn't have to endure another awkward second with Jason. At least, that's how she felt. He'd already attempted, yet again, to sneak a kiss in the restaurant after she reluctantly allowed him to slide onto her side of the booth.

Jason had just returned from the bathroom. "Mind if I scoot in?" He jerked his chin in the direction of the space adjacent to her.

It would have been rude to have denied him, so she gently slid over, anxiously rubbing her palms together, as if magically they would help soothe her nerves. Jason didn't seem to notice how on edge she'd been, her sheer desperation to steer the conversation away from anything that resembled a flirty approach, but he must have not caught the drift. Now, he was sitting right beside her, facing her and smiling with puppy eyes.

If she hadn't proved it earlier on, now she had to. As if from nowhere, she felt his fingers pushing a strand of hair from her cheek. It was the oldest trick in the book. Defensively, she had shuffled, bit her tongue as she forced a warm smile.

"You're very beautiful," he'd muttered, then as if it were as easy as one, two, three, he'd went in for the kiss. Thank God the waitress returned with the

bill, stopping Jason as easily as putting brakes on an emergency stop.

"Erm, sure," he replied, shrugging his shoulders. "I don't mind."

And that was that. Zack sat in the middle of the backseat, leaning his arms over each side of the front passenger and driver's seat. With the presence of Zack, Jason decided to remove the love ballad CD, opting to just return it to some radio station.

"So, did you have a good time tonight, Claire?" Jason asked. She instinctively glanced at the mirror on the visor, meeting Zack's amused eyes staring back at her own. *As if she needed I told you so,* she thought.

"Yes, I did," she replied, forcing her hand to clasp Jason's briefly as it rested on the gear stick.

There, she thought. She returned her gaze to Zack. *I don't feel anything towards you.* Forgetting that her action had consequences, she saw Jason's broadening smile from the corner of her eye.

It wasn't long till Jason was parked outside Claire's apartment block, bidding her farewell with admiration written all over his face, and Zack's pesky presence just a mere few steps behind her, attentively listening in.

"I had a *wonderful* night," Jason said. "Thank you for coming out with me. I hope we can do this again sometime."

Claire bit down on her tongue. She wanted to subtly drop the hint that they were just friends, but with Zack standing just a short distance away, and that nagging stubbornness, she opted to lie and flatter him adoringly, even if that meant giving him a kiss on his cheek.

"Bye!" She waved him off, shutting the door after she'd watched him walk towards the staircase. She closed her eyes as she sunk her head back on the door. *Shit, shit, shit.*

"Sounded like you *really* had a good night," Zack remarked. She opened her eyes; he stood there, chuffed to bits, folding his arms and leaning against the wall.

"I did," she insisted, walking towards the sofa.

"Sure, you did. *Oh, Jason! Oh, Jason! Fuck me, Jason!*" He mimicked her with a high, soft pitch and clapped his hands together enthusiastically. "Sure sounds like it," he added, returning to his calm, collected self.

"Oh, fuck off!" she cursed. "Not everything has to be about sex, you know! Who knows! I'd probably be getting it if your stupid ass didn't show up shouting my name down the road!" She aggressively attacked the pillow as she flopped down onto the sofa and crossed her arms.

"Babe, you know if my 'stupid ass' didn't show up, you would have been stuck in a car alone with a horny fella you don't even like," he said, kicking his feet up onto the coffee table as he sat down beside her.

"Idiot!" She pushed his shoulder. "You don't know that. Of course I like Jason. He's—He's—"

"He's what?" he interjected, flicking through the TV guide he'd picked up off the coffee table.

"Oh, just shut up! Why are you so irritating?" she snapped.

143

"Why can't you just confess that you're absolutely smitten with me? I'd gladly relieve the tension," he offered, holding his arms out as if he was suddenly beneath a beaming spotlight in the centre of a stage performance.

"No!" she spat, climbing onto her knees as she whacked the pillow on his arm several times. Zack grabbed the pillow firmly, not letting it loose, and said not a word. It stunned Claire for several seconds. They were beginning to feel like a trap, a spider laying its foundations for the ignorant fly to pass into.

Naturally, she pressed her lips together, a mechanism of defence to the swarm of butterflies inhabiting her stomach. His charcoal eyes hauntingly flicked back and forth, travelling to her own, then briefly halting at her lips. She grew impatient waiting for his next move. It was as if a cloud of mist had fogged her mind completely, and she knew searching for the appropriate solution was lost far beyond her reach. She knelt slowly, watching as he slowly leaned towards her, his lips travelling towards hers, frozen like a picture on a canvas. Claire must have stopped breathing; she could only hear her heart beat thumping through her ear drums. Whatever it was doing, it felt like it was frantically pumping thick volumes of excitement through her veins.

His left hand slid onto her cheek as he gently kissed her lips. Electricity simmered at their touch; she felt powerless and entirely at his mercy. *Why did he have this effect?* It pleased her more than it had frustrated her, a ratio she couldn't overthrow, knowing inside her stomach was doing backflips. She felt weakened on pure bliss. Claire expected more but grew disheartened as he pulled back.

She blinked several times. "Why—why did you stop?"

It was his turn to blink now. He almost choked. "What? Hang on, this is you we're—"

"Just shut up, already." She rolled her eyes as she aggressively smashed her lips against his. It became demanding, raw, and possessive as their mouths hungered for each other. She slid into his lap, feeling his needy hands grab her waist and slither towards the back of her neck as he tore away for air, tracing his lips at her collarbone. Claire fisted her hands into his shirt, grinding her body against him, dissolving completely into oblivion. Everything about him she wanted. The taste of alcohol from his tongue, the scent of his aftershave tickling her nostrils, and the body she wanted to worship. Their tongues slid teasingly against each other as he reclaimed her lips. She begged herself to stop, begged herself not to succumb to the weakness, but it was too much…her ass squeezed in the palm of his hand, his mouth, his *everything*.

There was just no stopping her. She gladly allowed him to guide her to lie back, his weight on top, not daring to stop as she wrapped her legs around his waist. Claire wanted it. She could feel it pressing into her. It was as if she'd been starved for days or walked a desert dehydrated, hallucinating water, till it materialised, and felt like honey dripping down her throat. How could she deny how horny she felt? *It was ludicrous!*

***

ZACK

Zack lifted his shirt over his head, urging her to counter-attack as his hands thumbed her thighs, steadying her as he spread them apart. He felt this could really happen. He felt anxious, exhilaration, possibly envious that she had been touched before, because every bit of him burned, the tip of his dick, the hairs upon his legs and arms as she groped his chest, feeling his abs, tasting his pec. Zack massaged her hips, slid his hands under her dress as he touched the waist line of her knickers. He had it. She kissed the side of his neck.

"Zaack," she panted.

He *had* it. The opportunity. She was hyperventilating at the skim of his lips on the inside of her hip. She *wanted* this. He *wanted* this. Yet he stopped.

She looked up, confused as he wet his bottom lip. What was wrong with him? *She wanted it. She isn't drunk. She's lying there for, you! What is wrong with you?* He pushed aside his thoughts. "We can't do this. I don't think…it's appropriate if we rush into things," he confessed, feeling utterly silly. He ran his hand through his hair as he sat back and sunk his head back. *This wasn't Zack. Zack went in for the kill. What's one woman got to do to suddenly change his mind?*

Claire didn't say anything as she sat up. The expression on her face was guilt, or it could have been anger, but he wasn't to know until she spoke. "I want to slap you...but," she muttered, looking down to her lap, "but I'm just as much to blame."

"I don't know why, but something is telling me no. And it's not my dick," he said.

She smiled a little at that before her face was replaced with an expression of sudden remorse. "Shit, this wasn't supposed to happen. What the fuck is wrong with me? I could have slept with you. Fucking hell."

"Hey, hey, less of the offence. Sex with me wouldn't equate guilt. *Trust me*," he defensively said, watching as she pushed her dress down. He placed a hand across her back, something he supposed would console her.

"Oh, man, what have I done?" she grumbled, dropping her head onto her knees.

"Well, unlucky, we haven't done anything. Like you said last time. Just forget about it. It never happened," he suggested. *How could he?* He sat in his trousers, the buckle undone and her body just seconds ago beneath his weight.

Claire sighed. "That sure sounds easy. Fuck...it would have been easier if it were Jason."

"Look." He swallowed his own pride. "Let's just, for this night only, just sit here. We'll allow this night to take its course, and by tomorrow morning, we forget this instance ever happened. I won't mention it again." He rubbed his jaw, feeling its stubbly surface brushing against his fingertips.

She looked hesitant at first. "Okay," she agreed as she slid back and rested her head comfortably onto his chest.

Something had made him stop. But what? Zack had never refused to sleep with a woman unless she didn't want it, but this time, something different had barred him from taking things further. What if they had slept together? What would have the consequences been? It's not like he could draw up a table with pros and cons, it was in the heat of the moment, and it had suddenly died as soon as he felt her melt beneath him. Nothing was making sense. She was willing, as was he. He liked to think she wasn't interested in Jason, but that suddenly changed. Would she rather it be him? Was he just the distraction? What was wrong with him? Now, with her resting against his chest, it felt like a responsibility to keep himself from her. What was this? *Sorcery?*

***

CLAIRE

What happened? First, she was mad, then she was climbing into his lap. She could have slept with him. She knew she had wanted it. But he stopped. She felt partly relief. As much as she liked to resist him, she knew that wasn't possible if she was encouraging the tension. And now Jason? She was fucking him over. For her own selfish, stubborn self, she'd perfectly encouraged someone, who Darren was convinced liked her from top to bottom, that she's madly into him too. There was no doubt about that. She had so many questions: why kiss him? Why? Why? And now lying next to him, she undoubtedly felt safe. But why? Why was the question, but never an answer.

CHAPTER TEN

CLAIRE

When daylight hit her face, her nose wrinkled as she squinted in discomfort, trying to escape its intensity, but it was no use. She was up. Turns out, they hadn't moved from the sofa, but now Zack was missing. It felt bare as she stretched her hands out onto the pillows. She flopped her arm across her forehead, sighing as she reflected over yesterday's mishap. She wanted to promise herself that she could start all over again today, because as much as she would love to erase yesterday, it was always gonna imprint her memories. There was no magical potion or device, or even vampires for that matter, to glamour her to forget. *Nothing.* So she knew she needed a fresh start.

Claire heard the front door go. She sat up, observing how Zack walked in, sweat cascading down his forehead, one earplug hanging down on his shoulder, and bare except for the blue basketball shorts hanging below his knees. She was a little alarmed by the sight. He seemed to force a smile.

"You're awake. Did you sleep okay?" he asked, pulling out the earplug as he placed his phone connected to the pair onto the kitchen counter. He went straight for the fridge, pulling out the orange juice and jugging down the carton.

"Yeah, er, where have you been? And what time is it?" she replied, awkwardly standing up as she brushed her hair from out of her face.

"Running. And it's eleven."

Claire nodded. He seemed a little absent-minded as he paced the kitchen a little, in and out of her sight from the doorway. "I thought you might have been a—"

"I thought it was probably best." He put the orange juice back, exited the kitchen, and paused. "I'm gonna go shower." Then he went.

Something didn't seem right. He seemed not as responsive as usual. Was he mad? But why? He'd stopped things. Or was he just annoyed he couldn't have a quick bang? Whatever was up his arse irritated Claire, more than it should have. She couldn't exactly barge into the bathroom unless she wanted another encounter, so she decided instead to make herself a coffee, knowing it could at least cheer her up a little.

***

ZACK

Zack got out of the shower, wiping the soap suds away from his ears as he sat on the edge of his bed.

He reflected as he looked at the deep blue duvet quilt, *somebody else used to have these sheets*. At least that's what she said when he'd borrowed them from the last occupant who owned this room. Was it a man? Did they question their actions when encountering *her*? It suffocated him. There was no fun masturbating in the shower when he knew he could have had the real thing yesterday.

He had brought his phone in, so he was thankful that when he collected it off the side table, Claire wouldn't have politely answered a call from his mother. "Hello, Mom," he greeted, balancing his phone on his right shoulder as he sprayed some deodorant under his armpit.

"You *haven't* forgotten about today, have you? I expected you half an hour ago," she replied, that patronizing tone running through his bones. He sighed. Zack had forgotten. His initial pause only made him imagine his mother with a scolding look.

"No, I haven't," he lied. "I just decided, as I usually do on a Sunday morning, to get up later. There's no harm in that, is there, Mother?"

"Tone, Zack. I'll see you in about half an hour or so. Traffic shouldn't be bad on the motorway." Then she ended the call.

Zack got dressed, opting for a white shirt and jeans combo, casual but formal. He would have to call Wickes, even if that bent the rules of the bet. His mother would question him if she witnessed him arriving in some unknown car. He opened his door, surprised to see Claire there, startled as she brought her hand down; it appeared she was just about to knock.

"I wasn't eavesdropping, I swear," she insisted. "I was just wanted to see if you were okay?"

"I'm fine. I'm going out, so I'll research that project we've got to do later," he said, a little abrupt he thought as he slid past her.

"Oh, will you be back later? I thought that we could cook roast dinner or something?" she suggested. "And don't worry, I'll teach you." She tried a smile.

He wet his bottom lip. "No, I'm out."

***

CLAIRE

It was rather strange. Not being alone on a Sunday, she'd been used to that since Abbey left. No, Zack's behaviour again. She tried to push the thought aside as she typed up the company's mission statement into PowerPoint. It was at least one step to polishing up their scribbled notes. As much as she hated the added work, she wanted to be passionate towards Project 42; at least it was an attempt to become more renewable in this polluted world. What changed the CEO's mind? Or what made him try again? The other project didn't work out, so why again? She could only guess; money wasn't a problem.

Shortly after, she decided to ditch the work; she had become suddenly attentive to dust showing on the TV stand. For most of the afternoon, she obsessively cleaned the apartment from top to bottom. She hoovered, washed up, polished, and took the trash out, even though the garbage bin wasn't full and the binmen weren't to show up till Wednesday. Maybe it was the bug of the "Sunday housework" that encouraged her to clean about.

Her mobile rang as she was just about to collapse onto the sofa. She grabbed it off the coffee table, falling back and answering. "Hello," she exhaled, kicking her feet onto the arm of the chair.

"Hey, it's me."

Jason.

"Oh, *hi,*" she responded, reluctantly trying to sound enthusiastic. She must have forgotten she had misled him last night. What else did she expect? For him to miraculously forget that she'd flirted with him at the final point of the night? *No.*

She should just come clean, tell him she's not interested, but how could she describe that without justifying that she did what she did to spite Zack, whom she was trying desperately not to *fall* for? *Fuck.*

"I had such a great night. I was just wondering if you're sure you want to do this again sometime. I like you, Claire. I really do. For quite some while now," he confessed, a long sigh of relief following after down the line.

Shit.

"Erm." She paused. *Okay, now or never. Confess or don't.* "Of course, wow, erm. I'm not—"

"Great, well, I'll plan for something else or whatever, but in the meantime, we can definitely take things slow. Oh, shit—I mean, sugar! I left the gas on. I should go. I'll see you at work tomorrow, bye!" Then he ended the call, leaving Claire in a desperate state of anxiety, shit-crazy, and wishing she had just been straight in the car. Why had she lied? Of course, she knew why. It was her stubborn reaction towards Zack, someone she didn't want to end up falling with, so it only made sense that her mouth, not her brain, defensively tackled the question. *Great job!*

***

ZACK

Zack's parents lived out in the countryside. Technically, they weren't exactly in isolation, they were pretty much living near the county town of Warwick, yet they still had rich access to sites of green, fresh air, and cow manure. It was his old home just as much as it was theirs. A country mansion with acres of land, it had been his home since his early adult years until he'd flown off to University.

He entered through the front door after passing their butler, Wilbur. The place lingered with memories: the red draping curtains made him reminisce of that time he'd snuck out a girl he'd slept with, and the large family portrait on the wall reminded him of the hassle they had to endure, standing there for hours as his father wanted a painted portrait placed above the fireplace wall.

Zack passed around the corner, heading towards the second large central room. His mother was dressed in a long, green, modest dress. She stood at the piano, something that barely got used, only on occasions. She was drinking from a glass of what he knew would be gin and tonic, a classic favourite of hers. She only liked to drink on Sundays.

"*Finally!* We've been waiting ages. What took you so long? Our kitchen staff had to halt, not knowing when you might show up." She frowned, placing her glass on a side table. "Has that shirt even been ironed? Look at you. Have a little pride, Zack," she lectured, pinching his sleeve as she studied his wrinkled shirt.

"Can we not, Mother?" he sighed.

"We will. You have a reputation to hold, one that appears non-existent at this point," she scolded. "You better get yourself in the dining room immediately. Your father needs to have another discussion with you, which you can only blame yourself for," she added, calling out then for a maid to attend to her.

Zack held his hands up in surrender before shoving them in his pockets as he headed into the dining room next door, a large space holding residence to a large oak table plastered with wine glasses, cutlery, and attended to by two nearby staff. There, as usual, at the head of the table, his father, Elijah Benson, wasted not a single glance at his son, who sat a couple chairs down from him. His father was too busy with the evening newspaper.

"Stop slouching. Sit up," he ordered, still not communicating with his eyes.

Zack couldn't really argue. His father could be an intimidating man, one he knew was a risky man to cross paths with. He sat up a little, resting his elbows on the table as he adjusted his watch strap.

Nothing was said. There wasn't even the chance before Jared showed up, trailing after their mother, holding a bouquet of flowers. He received affectionate kisses, a stern nod from their father, and then was invited to confer in some small talk. Between Zack and his father, however, you could hear a pin drop. Even the clatter and serving of food didn't seem to disperse the deadly silence. But then, his father was a man who didn't like to speak during most meals. He preferred to hold that business-like manner, contributing only when matters involved himself. It was their mother who took centre stage.

It was towards the end of the late evening when Zack was called into his father's parlour. Zack had always found the place quite intimidating from its oak surfaces, insufficient lighting, and the old grandfather clock in the corner of the room. It radiated power and wealth. His father poured himself a glass of liquor, something Zack's mother discouraged him to drink at the dining table. This was the time when the devil truly showed its colours. He'd witnessed, heard men cowardly falling to their knees in fear of Elijah Benson. But this was his father, a man he liked to think he wasn't afraid of. Heck, his father didn't know about Project 42. There was no reason to until plans were confirmed. Zack didn't want it to fail like last time and hear the constant nagging and lecturing of *I told you so*. This time it would be different; his father would be impressed.

His father's back was turned, but Zack could feel the deadly tension as he swirled the dark liquid around the glass. "You know," he began, slowly turning as he sat in the dark red chair. "I used to be proud of my decision when I saw my son carrying on the business. One generation to another generation. *But,*" he paused, the bitter sound of his teeth kissing together after swallowing a mouthful of liquor, "I never would have thought I'd be disappointed. I surely thought you might have learned from your last lesson, and yet you tarnished your own, but more importantly, my reputation at that gala. For your sake, Zack, you better be hoping you're not reconsidering those ideas of yours." His greyish brows launched up, the prevalent frown that appeared glued to his face 24/7 exerting only a little change as he held amusement within the depths of his eyes.

"Even if I was, hypothetically, I know what I'm doing," Zack said.

"But *do* you?"

"Yes."

A bitter laugh left his father's lips. "Hysterical. Really, Zack, you should have been a comedian."

Zack sighed. "Are we done here?"

"Just do what you're told, Zack. I don't want to be hearing, seeing, or even smelling a little investment going into one of those silly ideas of yours. We're a family-owned business, always have been, and the top of our league for private housing. Don't mess it up," he warned. "You're welcome to leave." He thrust his glass gently towards the door as he sat there triumphantly.

CHAPTER ELEVEN

CLAIRE

Once *again,* that bugger of an alarm clock was ringing incessantly. She tossed and turned, enraged that she could no longer sleep. It was a struggle and a half to kick the quilt off the end of the bed, and another great effort was needed to force herself to sit up and turn her phone's alarm off. Claire sat up, wiping away the coat of dribble before snagging a hair band off the side as she scrunched her hair into a messy bun.

Monday morning. Who doesn't love the first day of the week? The inconvenience of it being the day after the weekend. She was hoping Monday would at least mean some sort of a fresh start. Yet she knew that was far from the case.

Swinging her legs from her bed, she gradually stretched her arms, trying to ease the relentless ache pounding her all over. It eased as she stood up. She could barely keep her eyes open as she shuffled towards her door, then headed out into the open

159

hallway. There was not a sound inside the apartment except the birds chirping in the conifer tree next to the kitchen window.

She hadn't seen much of Zack yesterday; she wasn't even sure if he came back. It did bring some relief. At least, she didn't have to see him face to face. It was hard not to remember Saturday's chaos. As much as she would have loved to shift the blame to Zack, she knew that she was to blame this time around. She kissed him; she invited the trouble. *But why?* She had asked that several times yesterday.

Her feet sluggishly trudged against the pale beige carpet, heading for the bathroom door. Zack's door was still shut. *Thank God!* That sense of relief didn't last long when she heard noise emitting from the other side of the bathroom door. *The toilet flushing!* Oh, dear. So it appeared he was up. There was no time to retreat. The door opened inwards, Claire bit her tongue, and she could have screamed as some other person, not *Zack,* stood there.

"You're not Zack," she mumbled, indecisive in whether she needed to phone the police or run for her life. But she concluded she needed not to, considering the woman was wearing Zack's shirt, *only* Zack's shirt. She was putting Claire's pajamas to shame.

"Hi, I'm Casey," she said, her tone bubbly and friendly.

Am I getting stabbed in the stomach? Because it sure feels like it.

"You're *not*...Zack," she repeated, her tone evidently defeated.

The stranger giggled, her blonde tendrils of hair

bouncing off her shoulders. "No, not Zack. It's Casey. Zack's still asleep." She paused for a second or two, pushing her hair behind her shoulders before she asked, "Mind if I go make myself a coffee? I'm gasping."

"Erm, *sure.* Third cupboard on your left. Milk…is in the fridge and—"

"Great! I need to head off to work, so I'll be out of your hair in no time. Nice meeting you," she interjected, her smile appearing sinister towards Claire only as she headed towards the kitchen.

Okay, let's get this right, she thought. *There's a stranger in my house, and I've willingly allowed her to dally off into the kitchen.* But most importantly, why was Claire suddenly feeling very envious? Peed off? She didn't want to confess any of that. But actions still counted. Adjusting her spaghetti strap to push it back on her shoulder, she inhaled, then stormed towards Zack's door.

She knocked on it desperately. *"Zack. Zack. Get up."*

There was not a word. She did it several times more, paranoid to look down the corridor to see if the stranger was observing Claire's madman behaviour, but saw not a soul. It was useless. Zack was a heavy sleeper, something she'd noticed these past few days. With no other option, she opened the door, praying to God that he was decent. *Dear God.* She swallowed, unable to retract her eyes from the sight of his naked ass peeking from out of the covers. Claire felt like she had forgotten to speak. There was not a chance she could articulate a word at this moment.

He shuffled a little, stretching his arms forward as he brought the pillow closer. Each muscle upon his arms tensed. *Mother of cheese,* she thought.

"*Zack!*" she hissed, charging up to the side of the bed.

"Huh? What?" he groaned, refusing to let go of the pillow he cuddled.

"Who is *that* woman in my apartment?" she demanded.

"*Our* apartment," he exhaled. He was very reluctant to get up, yet he did, pulling the quilt over his lower half as he sat up and rested himself against the headboard. "She stayed the night. What else do you want me to say?"

Claire swallowed. It took no genius to see they'd slept together, but secretly she had hoped that wasn't the case. His words made it concrete. She was feeling irritated once again, and she wished to God to know why. She couldn't be jealous. Claire had made it clear Saturday that whatever happened was a mistake, and so did he. So why now? Why was her heart trying to jeopardise her brain's logical solution?

"*And?*" he persisted.

"And *what?*"

"What's the problem?" he asked. She was hesitant to answer. "You've come in here. You're aware that she's here, so I'll ask again, what's the problem? Do you have something to say?" A studious expression held his face captive. She felt very self-conscious as he continued to stare.

"There's no problem," she said through gritted teeth. "It just would have been nice to know that there was someone staying under *our* roof."

He chuckled. "And what? You like them to sign some sort of contract, or do I have to introduce them before I fuck? *Oh, hi, Claire. This is such and such. We're going to have sex now."*

"I don't mean it like that, *jerk face*," she spat.

Zack smiled with amusement, exhaling as he ran his hands through his hair.

"What's so funny?"

"Oh, I'm just curious as to why it bothers you so much," he replied.

"It doesn't. I couldn't care less."

"You're *jealous*, aren't you?" he said, cocking his head to the right.

"No." She shook her head as she crossed her arms. "Don't even start."

"Start what? You barged in here first."

"Err, excuse me." It was *her*. She entered the room, sweetly smiling as she carried a cup towards the bed and sat down. "Here, I made you some coffee." She passed it over to Zack, who accepted it, cupping it in his hands. "I hope I'm not causing you any trouble," she added, leaning her chin on Zack's naked shoulder.

"No, of course not," he replied, switching hands as he held the cup in one and slid the other around her shoulders. "No, my roommate, *Claire,* was just reminding me that you're very welcome here. Right, Claire?" he teased.

"Sure." She forced a smile.

***

CLAIRE

The journey on the bus couldn't have been more awkward. At least for *her,* anyway. Zack appeared not the slightest bothered as he sat beside her, looking at his phone between his legs. Her mind felt on fire. All those tiny cogs working overtime as she kept reflecting on this morning. Casey, or whatever her name was, had left not long after, but it didn't mean the pair had to keep it PG when they entered the living space, tangled up in one another, hands on each other, mouth on mouth. They could have suffocated each other. *But why do I care, anyway? Maybe because I desire his lips? No!* She shook the thought away. But in all seriousness, it was bugging her. The whole weekend had been a cock-up. She had Jason on a lead, she was kissing Zack like she'd forgotten her own morals, and he slept with someone else. She didn't know why she added the last point; he could sleep with whomever he wanted. She didn't care. At least, she thought she didn't.

They didn't speak as they got off and headed into the building. She was grateful for that as she wandered towards the office kitchen, meeting up with Darren, who stood at the counter stirring his tea and munching on chocolate biscuits. He hadn't heard her come in till she sighed, and immediately, like a turtle on a rocket, he eagerly sped on over towards the centre, sitting his bottom on the grey plastic chair.

"Claire, you wouldn't believe the news I have for you!" he said, leaning forward with a huge smile plastered across his little face.

She attempted to smile.

Darren clapped his hands. "Oh my *God*. The date was incredible. He bought me flowers, the meal was fabulous, and the chemistry was just there. Not once did I feel like I needed to pop off to the toilet to just waste time. I could barely breathe every time he looked me in the eyes!" His shoulders slumped as he dropped his head into his propped-up hands.

It didn't take effort this time to return a smile. She was genuinely happy for him. "*Wow,* that's so good, Darren. I'm glad you had a good time."

"I just feel so…alive with him. This is like the third date or so, and we're just clicking. It's incredible, really. You know I've never been into all that bullshit about love at first sight, but I'm feeling a little generous to the idea—okay, *really* generous. I think we're at the point now that we're ready to be in a relationship. I really want you to meet him, Claire," he said, reaching for her hand across the table and squeezing it.

"I really want to meet him, too." She squeezed his hand back before sliding to her side of the table.

"So, how was your date? I was right, though, wasn't I? It was a date." He took a sip from his cup.

"Yes, you were right," she sighed. "Turns out he's really into me. Like, *really.* Like, Darren, he was playing love ballads, for goodness' sake. *Love ballads.* He tried to kiss me several times throughout the night, and to make matters worse, I encouraged it towards the end. Don't ask." She shook her head, refusing to share the information about Zack's presence in all of this.

"Wow, shit. That does sound chaotic. I'm sorry it didn't work out as planned. Or that it was a date. But wait. You encouraged him? What do you mean?"

"I…guess I felt bad," she lied.

"Well, shit."

"Claire, hey," someone interjected. *Jason.* He approached the table, smiling as he held his hand across her left shoulder. "Could we talk?"

She blinked at Darren. Whatever he wanted to discuss, she knew it was something about the date, something she could have made herself very clear on if she hadn't flirted back. She could now have the chance to set things right.

She nodded, getting up and grabbing her bag off the table as she followed Jason, who'd decided the conversation was best held in the emergency staircase. *Déjà vu*, for sure. She shuddered as she tried not to reflect on that moment gnawing at her heart. What she needed to focus on was getting through this at exactly half-past eight in the morning, half an hour before she officially started work.

"So." He blushed. "I have to say it again. I really had a good time. I mean, forget the film and food. It was you that really made the night. I-I, really—"

"Jason, I need to say something," she interrupted, biting the inside of her cheek, knowing she was going to full well crush him to the core. "I don't—" She stopped. She was looking out the small window in the emergency door that led back into the office. At that moment, her anxiety spiked on edge as she saw Zack heading straight for them.

What the fuck, she thought. She didn't know why, but something pushed her to change her attitude.

It was so strategic as she heard the door being pushed open; she leaned forward and smacked her lips against Jason's. Then she pulled back.

"Oh, my bad."

She looked at Zack, tasting her bottom lip. Was that disappointment on his face? She didn't know, but he soon turned, pushing the door open as he went back in. *Fuck, fuck, fuck. What was she doing?* Instead of fixing the giant hole, she knew she only made it worse because her attention was soon brought back at Jason fondling her hand. *Shit.* He looked like a puppy high on life. She kissed him. And for some reason, she knew it had to be because of Zack. *Why?*

"Well," he muttered, lovesick in the eyes. "I was not expecting that." His thumb was still stroking her hand.

"Erm, could you excuse me one moment?" she said, pressing her lips together as she slipped her hand away from his, desperately trying to escape what felt like a small room closing in on her.

"So, another date?" he called after her.

"Yeah, sure." She nodded, urgently opening the door as she sped past the row of cubicles and past groups of people as she headed for her own, questionably safe, one. She exhaled, slamming her bag on the desk as she scrunched her eyes closed and cursed to herself. *Shit, shit, shit.* What had she done? That was not fixing. That was making the problem worse. *Idiot.*

Someone cleared their throat from behind her.

She turned in her chair, acknowledging Zack as he leaned his hand on top of the cubicle wall, something she wouldn't have been able to do at her height.

"Zack. W-where's your chair?" she asked, registering that his side of her desk wasn't occupied.

"Graves found me a spare cubicle a few rows ahead. After all, our mentoring is done. I just came to tell you that Graves has assigned each group a spare office on floor ten to prepare the presentation. We're in room A34," he informed her, barely making eye contact as he looked elsewhere, mainly around the office.

"Oh, well, wait for me. I'll just grab my bag and whatnot," she replied.

Was he mad? He didn't exactly look too pleased. But why would he care? He was with a woman this morning, and she, well, she mistakenly kissed Jason.

Claire collected any necessary things she might need, including the memory stick she'd saved some of the PowerPoint presentation on. Anything else, like a computer, would be provided. She wasn't even feeling that awkward sharing an office alone with him. He waited as asked, and not too long after, they were standing some distance away from each other as the buttons lit up at each floor they passed.

Zack headed out first. Room A34 wasn't far at all. It was the third room on the right, straight down the corridor. Claire could see the other familiar faces that made up one of the groups entering a room further down. Graves had made it clear that not every group would be presenting, only one would represent the company, but the variety made it easier for options. Theirs was primarily focused on sales; the marketing team had their selected few who would eventually combine with whoever was chosen to present. That made Claire a little more vexed. She could be doing all this work only to find their presentation would not be needed, and that time invested would be wasted.

He entered the day code, a four-numbered pin that saved the expense of having to use a key. He opened the sturdy door. Inside, it was a simple grey and black meeting room holding a large beige oval table in the centre with several black office chairs surrounding it and a television screen on the opposite wall. The primary function of these rooms was for conference meetings or group work. Claire had been up here several times in her position. She'd presented and discussed with clients alongside her peers and participated in monthly meetings in the department on budget costs between the sales and marketing teams effectively set by the accounting department.

Oddly, he seemed to know where everything was kept. He knew laptops were in the laptop trolley on charge at the back of the room and knew the room had its own storage cupboard stocked full of stationary, like paper, A3 to A4. She didn't say a word.

"So, erm," she said, shuffling her feet on the spot.

He ignored Claire as he opened a laptop and sat

down. He connected it to the television wirelessly, bringing up a pie chart with percentages. "We've already discussed as a pivotal point towards persuading the council that our product can be redefined towards those within the area by age. New home buyers, younger or even retired folk, as shown here." He moved the cursor over the green segment on the pie chart. "These are our targeted customers that we've proved are geographically located within the area. We should definitely add this to the presentation, and I think if this project does go ahead, we inform the marketing team to up their focus on these groups. Reach out to new buyers—"

"Wow, Zack. Breathe in some air, at least," she cut in. "Let's just take this step by step." She slowly sat down opposite him.

"I would, but this is some important shit to persuade the council that they're doing right by investing in our product," he replied snarkily.

"Zack, I think you should chill a bit. We're only creating a presentation. We're not solving world hunger," she replied, feeling a little on edge.

He exhaled. "I just want to do this right. It's important for me—I mean, the business. I need to make a good impression. This is my first huge project as part of the team." He shuffled in the chair.

"I know, I understand. Just chill a bit," she calmly said, hoping he would ease a little. Part of her was wondering if he was so uptight because of just witnessing her smacking lips with Jason.

***

ZACK

It was obvious he was pissed off. Zack wasn't sure why. Of course, he did. He'd stumbled on Claire getting cozy with that Jason. It vexed him. Surely, it was a little insensitive for Claire, considering they'd kissed there. It was the first time he'd shut her up, given her exactly what she wanted, what she needed. And this weekend? He had no part to blame in that. After all, something had insisted he stop things before they escalated. What was that? The rational part of his brain? And now this rational part, he believed, was making him behave almost scandalously. He felt deeply hurt seeing Claire all puppy eyes with that fella. *Why?* Zack had no clue. The feeling he had was preposterous!

Look at her, he thought. Those brown, wild eyes, tender, kissable lips, and that body he'd yearned for. *Listen to her.* She was babbling on, trying to discuss what they needed and what they should slice out of the presentation. He wasn't listening; he was too busy observing how her mouth moved, imagining her suddenly talking dirty.

"You had me right where you wanted, Zack. Why not just take me now?" she moaned, fisting her hands into her hair as she grinded herself up and down on the chair. What was this? Wild fantasy?

He blinked. The image dispersed. She wasn't moaning nor was she on about sex.

"So I think we should cut this." She pointed at

the scribbled note on the mind map they'd produced last Friday. "This isn't necessary. We should just focus on how the product is going to produce profits for the council. This just reflects our own requirements to improve efficiency between marketing and sales. What do you think?"

He blinked again.

"Zack?"

***

CLAIRE

Zack didn't even appear responsive. Was he even listening? That was the question. Claire sat a little back, wondering when on earth he'd reply. It was a little longer than she expected until that mouth began to move, but it wasn't entirely what she'd expected to come out.

"Would you have really been disgusted if we'd had sex that night?" He shrugged his shoulders, dead-ass serious as he looked directly at her.

"Err, this isn't the conversation we should be having. You said we weren't gonna talk about that," she mumbled, anxiously pushing a strand of hair behind her ear that had come loose from her ponytail.

"Why not? Is it because of that new boyfriend of yours?"

"He's...not my boyfriend," Claire defended herself, trying to appear more interested in the laptop screen than what was coming from out of his mouth.

"Sure." He shook his head as he began to roll the pencil beneath his fingers.

Claire was irritated. "You can't exactly say anything. What about you and that woman this morning? Is she your girlfriend? Or is she just some fuck buddy?"

"That's got nothing to do with us," he replied, shrugging her comment off.

"And Jason has nothing to do with you, either. We're not talking about this anymore," she said, grabbing a pen.

"Well, I sure as hell want to," he objected, sitting up a little straighter.

"And I don't," she hissed. "It was a mistake."

"A mistake? *Really?*" He chuckled without an ounce of humor.

"Yes."

Zack stood up, calmly walking around the table over to her. She didn't say a word and refused to stop gripping the pen in her hand. He grabbed a hold of the left arm of her chair and spun her aggressively to face him. He held her there, holding her eyes as he leaned a little closer in. "So, you're telling me," he quietly said, "that you kissing me was a mistake?" Zack cocked his head to the right.

"Y-es," she meekly said.

He gently cupped his right hand under her chin, stroking his thumb across the surface. Zack wet his bottom lip and slowly leaned in. He paused, his eyes directly capturing hers. His lips softly kissed hers, catching her startled breath as she closed her eyes. She wished him to deepen it, but he chose not to, pulling back.

"If it was a mistake, you wouldn't be breathing like you are, nor would you be willingly allowing me to taste your lips," he muttered, releasing his hand. Zack composed himself, acting as if nothing happened as he walked back around to his chair. "And yes, I agree with what you said. Keep the presentation relevant."

Claire exhaled shakily.

He was messing with her mind. Whatever was rational appeared illogical. Whatever was right seemed wrong. Whatever was wrong felt right. Whatever she didn't want to do, she did.

She slowly turned in her chair. He wasn't even looking at her; he was looking at their notes, scribbling dotted notes down. How was he so calm? How was he just sitting there? What the fuck was wrong with him? Claire felt insane. She couldn't even think properly. Deep down, she knew that nagging throb below was beckoning him. *God,* it was driving her crazy.

Fuck's sake, she thought. As if that kiss with Jason could ever compare. She didn't feel any toe curling, no magical sensation; it felt like nothing. But Zack, sitting opposite her, suddenly made worlds combine, made her feel like she was lacking oxygen.

Claire stood up. She didn't argue with her feet. She walked around and grabbed his tie as she forced him to acknowledge her. He did, sitting there, bewildered but not entirely stupid as he spread out his legs further, giving her the space to sit on his lap. She wasn't thinking. *What is two plus two?* God, she couldn't even say. That cologne? It sent her hormones crazy.

She grabbed his cheeks as she kissed him, intoxicated all over again. He didn't object, holding his hands around her back as he pulled her closer in. Claire had no control as she grinded herself on him, sliding her hands through his hair as she thrust her own tongue deeper into his mouth. The chair squeaked when she moaned as his hands squeezed her ass. Each fingertip sent her insane; it burned through to the flesh. Claire was no stranger to his member as she felt it, rubbing it with her right hand. She couldn't even remind herself that they were at work. There was no stopping her.

Hearing him groan through his teeth as she continued to rub him made her want it more.

Then there was a knock on the door.

Claire froze, her lips wet, her knickers wet. She jumped off, flattening her hair down. Thank God these walls weren't glass. She didn't mutter a word as she headed to the door, observing how Zack bit his lip as he shuffled about, supposedly trying to get rid of that boner.

She exhaled and checked herself over again before opening the door.

It was one of members of the other group.

"Hi." They smiled. "Have you got any spare paper?"

Chapter Twelve

CLAIRE

It was possibly the worst thing she could have done. As if she needed to be reminded that once again she had started it. They hadn't spoken after it happened—in fact, she swore to herself that it wouldn't happen again. Claire refused to talk about it, so for the rest of that week, she distanced herself. Or *tried* to. They still lived together and had to work together on the project. The event was brushed under the carpet just like the others. It didn't mean *shit*.

However, as much as she tried, something always seemed to crop up. There was the bathroom incident later that same week. Claire was in the bathroom bathing, and quite peacefully too. She added a bath bomb, set her playlist on her phone, then succumbed to the peaceful serenity of water against her skin. At that time, Zack wasn't home, and she'd expected to have at least two hours before his arrival—Zack was going to the gym more often that week. She was perhaps twenty minutes in the bathtub, her eyes closed, the distant sound of melody in the background, when out of nowhere the bathroom door abruptly opened. Zack entered: ear-plugs in, sticky sweat against his forehead, and then the worst—a mischievous grin framing his face. Claire screamed, sitting up and covering as much as she could.

"You motherfucker!" she remembered shouting. Then she demanded he cover his eyes as she tried to reach for the towel hanging off the side.

"I *did* call out," he had said, facing the door. "Promise I didn't see anything—on second thought, though…"

Nothing seemed to work. Zack was even intruding into her dreams. She would dream of the recent paragraphs she'd read from a romance book, some cliché cowboy and country girl falling for one another, and then out of nowhere, her mind would slap Zack's face on the man. It was *actually* hysterical the way her mind planned things: marriage proposals, hot sex, feisty make outs. No matter what she tried to do, she couldn't get him out of her head.

It was Friday. Another week had gone by so quickly. It wasn't even a little less awkward. Two weeks he'd been in her life and he'd already stomped over it like a baby elephant. It was a lot for one to go through.

They'd finished pretty early, rounding up their final points for the third slide. The presentation was coming along all right. Zack was actually incredibly helpful at times, and as a means of trying to grip her own sanity, anytime they were left alone in that office, she refused to participate in any eye lingering. *Bad choice.* She didn't want last week's chaos. And more importantly, they had deadlines to meet.

Zack had been moaning all evening, rubbing his stomach, craving food.

"I'm fucking hungry," he moaned once again. Claire was browsing through her social feed on her phone, refusing to give him the slightest bit of sympathy until he suggested they go out to eat. "I'll pay."

He didn't seem to know exactly where to go, so with a bit of encouragement from Claire, they chose a gastro pub in the centre of the city, not far from the cinema she'd ventured to on her date last Saturday which, speaking of, was painfully nagging her. Jason was persistent, appearing every time she walked in the office's kitchen, sat in the canteen, or walked outside for a breath of air. The only peace and quiet she got was through the remainder of the day with the devil himself, Zack.

"So pick what you like. Meal is on me," Zack said, sitting inches away from her in the round booth. He had his arm draped around the back, looking over her shoulder as he looked at the menu sitting in front of her. Claire was studying it, her mouth watering.

"There's *too* much to choose from," she confessed.

"Oh, the choices, choices. What a hard life," he sneered, snatching the menu from her.

"Hey!"

"I think I know what I'm having," he said, ignoring her squirm of disapproval.

"Well, I would have, but you snatched it from me, you pig," she replied, taking it from his hands as she tried again to study the menu. "Blimey, that chicken and BBQ sounds nice. Hm, I really like that other one though as well." She pointed at the picture. Her stomach growled like mad.

"Well, how about you have that?" He pointed at what she was considering. "And then, say, me for dessert?" he suggested with a coy smile. There was that boyish charm scuttling with her heart. It's that *smile*. That was the secret ingredient. Every time it appeared, it made her knees wobbly.

She blushed. "Shut up," she hissed, rolling her eyes. "I thought we weren't *ever* discussing that."

"We never agreed to anything. Lighten up. I'm not actually expecting you and me to do shit." He fingered the fork between his fingers before tapping it gently on the oak table. She was looking at it, almost mesmerised.

"Anyway—" he began, sitting up a little.

"Can I ask something?" she interjected, toying with the watch around her right wrist.

"Sure." He looked directly at her.

"Would I—actually," she shuffled a little around on the spot, sliding her hands under her thighs, "be the type you'd go for?" she asked, anxiously biting her inner cheek.

"Truthfully, no," he responded, thanking the waitress who returned with their drinks. "But," he added, "it's good, if you get me."

"Oh, well, that doesn't mean I'm interested, so—

" She stopped as she picked up her pint of cider and knocked a little back, instantly regretting her decision.

"I didn't say you were. Besides, I thought it wasn't something you wanted to discuss."

"It isn't," she agreed quickly. "I just was— actually, never mind." She paused for a second or two, awkwardly clenching her hands around the pint glass. "So, erm."

"Well, let me ask you a question. Do you genuinely even like that Jason? Because it's considered odd if you're kissing another guy," he said, sipping his pint of amber-coloured beer.

She pressed her lips together. "Of course I do," she lied. "I just haven't been thinking straight when I'm around you. I think you're just so good at manipulating me when you—"

"When I what?" he interrupted.

"I don't know." She shrugged her shoulders. "Let's just forget about it."

"Fine."

"Fine."

The waitress returned eventually, taking down their orders and leaving the pair in dead silence.

Zack broke it, as if he'd used a knife and sliced through thin air. "You know there's no shame if you just admit that you're into me. I get it. I'm just that likeable of a character. It's a first, I'll admit. Not a single woman has denied it, but I get it. You just don't want to come across as desperate," he said, cocking his head to the right.

"Pssf," she snorted. "I do not *like* you. A vain person like you? No chance. Actually, you know, come to think of it, maybe it's because I'm teasing you. A taste of your own medicine, huh?" She picked up her glass and swallowed another mouthful.

"Oh, *really?* Teasing me? My, you should have been an actress then, because you're pretty good at trying to prove me otherwise." He slid his hand through his hair as he shuffled a little further back into the seat.

Claire bit down on her tongue.

He smirked. "What? Cat got your tongue?"

"N-o. I'm just thinking...that you're just a conceited man. And yes, I'm teasing, because if you think for a second I'll ever have sex with you, ha! Think again! Not every woman wants to bow down at your feet," she replied, sitting forward as she held the rim of the glass kissed to her bottom lip.

"Who said anything about sex? I'm just simply pointing out that you've been pretty eager these last few times to begin shit with me. Did I? No, I didn't." He held his hands up in surrender.

Claire frowned. "I told you, I'm teasing you."

"What is it? First, you're saying I'm manipulating you, and now you're teasing me? I'm just saying you're not exactly convincing me, or yourself for that matter," he argued, propping one leg over the other.

"Eurgh, just sssh!" she grumbled, taking another huge mouthful of cider. She knew she'd regret it if she didn't slow down. But it became apparent she wasn't thinking about that; she was thinking more about the man sitting next to her, who was making her feel like she was going bonkers.

"Aye, aye." He shrugged his shoulders.

"I mean for real," she interjected, not remaining hushed herself, nor willing to side-track off the subject. "Have you even been in a committed relationship? Or do you just think every woman wants to sleep with you?"

"First, no. Second, I don't, I just know," he replied earnestly.

"Well, I have news for you, they don't," she objected, then she continued, flustered and highly vexed. "And really, you shouldn't feel good about it. That Casey, or whatever her name is, hasn't called back. Clearly, you're using her like she's using you." She then proceeded to take another mouthful of cider.

"Actually, here." He presented her his phone, revealing the several messages underlined under the name of a phone number. "And that's the point of casual sex," he calmly said, "so, chill. Are we done?"

"Yes. Actually, no. You know what, yeah, I'm leading you on. I'm kissing you because one of these days, you'll fall for me, and then I'll drop you, and you'll see what it's like—I tell you, watch it." Claire waved her hand aggressively about, slouching as she already regretted drinking half of the cider.

The waitress arrived, setting down their meals. Zack had only a second to figure out a reply, though he really didn't need one with the state Claire was in.

"Is that right?" he replied, cutting into his steak drizzled with peppercorn sauce.

"Yes." She glared at him. "I don't kiss because I like it—no!" She hiccupped. "You don't even kiss nice. I just do it 'cause I'm leading—" Claire hiccupped again.

"Okay, okay, eat your food before it gets too cold, and I suggest we order you a glass of water, you lightweight." Zack took charge as he ushered the waitress over.

"Whatever." She hiccupped.

Later that evening, she was stacked up against two pillows, arm over her face as she rested her eyes. It couldn't have been more awkward, knowing you were full-on drunk—a lightweight—from just one glass of cider. What was she even saying? Claire wasn't that gone because she remembered every little detail. She even remembered receiving the text message from Jason and flashing it off in Zack's face as she agreed to another date this Saturday, something she immediately once again regretted. Who was she fooling? The Pope?

"Here, have this," Zack said, interrupting her thoughts. She sat up, groggily rubbing her eyes as she accepted the glass of water from his hands. "Maybe next time, keep off the cider." Zack then sat on the opposite couch, grabbing the remote control from off the side as he switched on the television.

"I bet you're loving every moment of this," she said.

"Of what?"

"Just this evening. Since day one. You think I don't mean it, but I do," she explained.

"I have no idea what you're on about."

There was a knock on the front door. Three hasty knocks followed after.

"I'll get it," she told him, getting up to her feet. "After all, this still is my apartment."

She weakly walked towards the door, feeling tired and a little dizzy. Claire opened it.

"Abbey?"

Chapter Thirteen

CLAIRE

"Abbey?" she reiterated, blinking twice, maybe three times. Yet who else could it be? Who else could rock a short, bright red pixie cut bob and black cat eyeliner with red lipstick? The only rivalry towards her identity would have to be the horrendous pink leggings matched with a pair of thick red socks, a blue one-shoulder top sparkling with dozens of costume sequins, and green clogs—something Claire was confident the Abbey she knew wouldn't put together. She looked as if she'd had a fight with her wardrobe.

Her face was stained with black smudges of mascara. Abbey's blue eyes shifted from Claire's to behind her shoulder, implying that Zack wasn't too far behind. Claire didn't say a word as she grabbed her jacket with the fluffy hood and shoved on a pair of her trainers sitting near the side of the door.

"Let's go talk outside," she instructed, holding her hand out as she guided Abbey back the way she came. They walked down the stretch of corridor, passing the doors of her neighbours; number 49 always had their television on loud, and number 48, Abbey had once joked she heard the neighbour playing porn. It didn't seem, though, that Abbey was in the mood for reminiscing.

Taking the short flight of stairs, they reached the ground floor, and Claire steered Abbey towards the back door fire exit into the shared communal car park. Abbey still hadn't said a word as she looked towards a patch of weeds growing through the gap in the broken tarmac.

"So, what happened? I mean, I love that you're here, but it's not a good sign when you're showing up looking uncoordinated with tears in your eyes. What happened, Abbey?" she asked, placing a hand across her friend's back.

Abbey exhaled shakily. "We had an argument. I accused Ryan of cheating. I thought I saw messages from that woman he'd told me he knew from college and met at the gym. I was just going on his phone to check the time when I saw she'd messaged him. She'd put all this stuff asking him if he was with someone, putting kisses all here and there. I started going off, not even acknowledging that he made it clear he was in a relationship until he showed me the message again. I felt embarrassed, so I left, coming here. It took me twenty minutes in the car to get here, and all I've been thinking is how stupid I've been. What if—if he leaves me or something? I should have trusted him." She threw her hands in the air.

"Aw, Abbey," Claire cooed, pulling her friend

into her arms.

"He's—he's been phoning me all night. I'm just too scared to face him right now." She sniffled, wiping a tear from her cheek as she pulled back from their affectionate embrace.

"Honestly, Abbey, I know Ryan wouldn't be the one to cheat. He'll understand that you're just upset, that's all. Stay tonight, and then tomorrow, sort it out with him," Claire offered.

"I just feel like an idiot. I acted like an insecure teenager. I shouldn't have barged out like I did. It's just so unusual for us. We always talk things out. And I...failed this time." She held her face into her hands.

"Now, come on. Tomorrow, you'll talk things over and you'll feel a lot better. Let's get you inside now," Claire encouraged as she opened the door that led back into the apartment block. "And I know arrangements are a little different now, seeing as your room is occupied, but I'm sure we can work something out."

That was probably a good excuse; as unfortunate as this was for Abbey, having her friend back for the night made any possible encounters between herself and Zack a little less possible.

"So, where is he?" her friend piped up, scanning the central room and the bits of the kitchen she could see from where they stood.

"I don't know," Claire replied, shrugging her shoulders as she guided Abbey towards the sofa. "Instead, let's get you seated, and I'll make you a cup of tea." She squeezed Abbey's shoulder encouragingly.

Claire headed into the kitchen, feeling nostalgia tug as she pictured Abbey balancing on a chair trying to reach the secret supply of wine she used to stash behind the packet of crisps and bottles of vinegar. It would be so much easier if Abbey hadn't moved out.

She was leaning on the counter as the kettle boiled when she suddenly heard voices in the living room. There were two other living souls in the apartment, which meant it could only mean Zack was talking to Abbey, or vice versa. Either way, she wasn't too sure she liked leaving Abbey on her own, for her own safety, and whether he'd find it funny to slip a few details, here and there, of how Claire had her tongue down his throat.

She quickly poured hot water in the mug, added the tea bag, and stirred it before splashing a dollop of milk in there. She hurried back into the central room. There he stood, as if on cue, that charm radiating from his head to toes, and that smile, lighting up thousands of beacons. It made her toes clench as she observed Abbey's miracle change in attitude. She was playfully flirting back, constantly tugging her hair behind her ears, and blushing as if she hadn't just walked into the apartment, bawling her eyes out.

"Abbey, here's your tea," Claire interjected, gripping the handle as she barged in front of Zack and gave her friend the mug. She stood back up, glaring at Zack discreetly.

"Claire, you didn't tell me you had such a *hunk* living under your roof," she teased, cupping the mug in her hands as her eyes did a once over on him. Zack smirked blatantly. It was actually sickening to think her friend was undressing him right now with her eyes, and under the circumstances, Claire thought it right to divert her off those tracks.

"Err, Abbey, maybe you could message Ryan now to tell him you're at mine," Claire suggested, hoping the hint of his name might push her interest off Zack. This wasn't out of jealousy, she reminded herself; this was to protect Abbey.

"Nah, he'll be fine. I'd rather he didn't. I'll phone him in the morning," she said, ignoring Claire as she continued to coyly undress Zack. "Anyway, your roommate, Zack, has already offered to share his bed."

Claire could have choked.

"I don't at all mind sleeping on the couch," he added, dampening the vivid image running around her mind by just a little.

"No, no, Abbey, you can share my bed. Zack can have his own. There's enough room for both of us, I'm sure," she stated.

Abbey sighed before taking a mouthful of tea. "Wait, did you put any sugar in this?"

***

Claire was tossing and turning on her side of the bed. If there was anything she didn't miss about Abbey, it was her incessant snoring. *Seriously!* The woman could snore through a hurricane or topple the sound of a rock band head moshing with its audience. It was barely half one in the morning, they'd only gone to sleep fifteen minutes ago after once again going over Abbey's situation with Ryan, and already she was fast asleep. Claire had, however, managed to persuade Abbey to text Ryan, just to let him know where she was. But for now, there was no way she was getting a blink of sleep.

She sat up, dragging herself off the bed as she tip-toed over to the door. The couch seemed more appropriate than ever. It would have been all right if it was like how it used to be; two walls and two doors once separated the pair. She gently opened the door and closed it behind her. The corridor was dark, and her fingers fumbled about on the wall, trying to find the switch. *Click.*

Thank God, she thought. Claire felt uneasy standing alone in the dark.

There was already a red blanket on the couch, so she hadn't to worry about searching through her room for it. She climbed onto the couch, thankful the other light switch was just arm's length from the end of the sofa on the wall, switched it off, and then laid back. Not a peep of sound.

Click.

Claire opened her eyes, heart thumping through her ears, and defensively held the blanket to her chin. She didn't know karate, but she knew where to aim, depending on the sex. Thoughts rallied in her head: *Did she lock the front door? Was the apartment haunted? Was there a mass murderer in the living room seconds away from stabbing a knife into her forehead?*

She held her breath.

"What are you doing on the couch?"

190

Claire looked up. They were now towering above her.

"Bloody hell, Zack. You frightened the life out of me," she sighed, sitting up as she dragged the blanket around her shoulders.

"Sorry, I didn't expect someone to be asleep on the couch. I thought you were sharing your room with your friend?" he asked, scratching his left shoulder. She didn't even feel the need to comment that he was naked from the waist up, those abs shining like some treasure chest unearthed from the ground.

"No," she mumbled. "She snores really badly, so I opted for the couch. What are you doing up?"

"Glass of water."

They didn't say anything as he went into the kitchen, returning with a full glass. Claire was trying to get comfortable, whacking the cushion to plump it up.

"You could always come to bed with me," he offered.

Claire hissed as she turned to face him, like an arrow hitting a bullseye. "How dare you! I most certainly will not!"

Zack stepped back, holding his hands in surrender, still wretched with a self-satisfied grin. "Babe, I didn't mean it like that. I was offering for you to sleep on the one side. I don't snore. You can even create some sort of barrier between us, but...come on—this couch isn't comfortable."

"I'm not sleeping in the same bed with you," she bitterly refused.

She tried.

Ten minutes later, she was knocking on his door. The couch was truly uncomfortable. She had probably tried every body position humanly possible. It was either too hard in some places or the dip in the middle prevented her body from spreading evenly across the surface.

"My, my...if it isn't the woman who said she wouldn't share a bed with me," he teased, resting his arm on the side door frame. She didn't say a word as she slipped under his arm, entering the room.

"Don't try anything," she said as she headed for the bed. Zack gently closed the door, ogling Claire as she fought with his bed to best fit her standards. She split it in half with one of the pillows.

"Now," she exhaled, sitting up to rest her hands on her hips. "You stay on your side, and I'll stay on mine."

"You're the boss," Zack replied, amused. "Whatever you say."

Slipping into her half, she huffed as she pulled over the duvet, instantly washed with the familiar scents that were Zack: mint shampoo and his usual cologne. Anxiety soon began to crawl over her skin, dawdling at every inch, waiting for him to join her in bed. Claire wanted to peek, yet she somehow suspected his heated glance would reach hers. *What is taking him so long?* she thought, hugging the duvet further. *And why am I so impatient anyway?*

"Sweet dreams," he finally said as she felt the other half dip. Not even then did the swarm of butterflies settle at her core, nor did sleep confront her.

Another ten minutes in and she was even more restless than she was before. It was all because she knew Zack was right next to her.

Sighing, she turned on her back, flopping her arms out to the side of each other. A bead of sweat threatened to break out on her forehead. How was she going to survive the night? How?

"Can't get to sleep?" Zack mumbled in the darkness. Even the rough edginess in his tone crawled beneath her skin. What else would she get turned on by? The sound of him peeing? *Goodness gracious! Get a grip!*

"No," she said truthfully.

"Well, me neither," he exhaled, then she felt him shuffle as he turned on the bedside lamp.

Claire felt her eyes being squelched from the light flooding the room. "What are you doing?"

"So, what do you want to talk about?" he replied, leaning his head on his arms propped up on the pillow.

"I don't want to talk about anything. I just want to sleep," she mumbled.

Alarm bells started ringing as soon as she felt the barrier being lifted. She turned on her side. "What! Hey!" she hissed. "What are you doing? Put it back. It's there for a reason."

"Well, I want to see your face," he muttered. He was now lying on his side, looking directly at her.

Claire blushed.

"Why do you always look at me like that?" he asked. "Like you want to throw knives in my face?"

"Because I do."

Zack didn't say a word; his eyes were glued to

hers.

His finger brushed her bottom lip. *Not a word.* She was fully intoxicated.

"My turn," he uttered gently.

Claire braced herself, eagerly watching as Zack leaned over towards her.

***

ZACK

He rested his left hand beside her on the pillow, observing how her hazel-coloured eyes shifted between his own, anticipating what she was to do next. To be honest, he didn't know what he was doing, and it felt like he was being commanded by a puppeteer rather than his own actions. It was like dipping his finger in a jar of honey—Claire was so sweet and yet a dangerous addiction.

***

CLAIRE

Her chest rose swiftly at Zack's descent towards her soft, plump lips. At an instant touch, a scintillation of lust drove through, daring Claire to move in closer and, with relish, fondle his naked torso. The need for each other was transparent. Urgency burned through them both. Their lips moved further in a hot synchronization as Zack pushed her further down into the bed. Zack rolled on over to straddle himself upon Claire, trying to repress the hunger by deepening the kiss. An agreeable moan left her lips as he gently tugged on her bottom lip with his teeth.

"Zack."

Her hands impatiently moved towards the waistband of his bottoms. Zack stopped them as he grasped them both, planting them to either side of her head as he brushed his lips against the side of her neck. "Ssssh," he responded. "I don't understand...but for once I ain't listening to my dick. Claire...you don't understand how badly I want to fuck you right now, but I won't. I...can't." He was still smothering his lips upon her neck. He stopped.

She held her breath as he flopped back onto his side.

"I get it," she whispered.

He didn't need to say anything as she turned and slipped herself under his welcoming arm. Oddly, as much as she wanted to explain, it made sense. Her heart knew but wouldn't confess.

Chapter Fourteen

CLAIRE

Dribble emanated from the corner of her mouth. She was hugging something brawny, and she didn't want to move a muscle.

"Morning." The sound sexily sashayed into her ear drum.

She smiled, hugging tighter. *Blink.*

"Oh, *shit,*" she cursed, letting go.

Zack stretched his arms as he sat up. "You might want to consider leaving soon. I hear people get the wrong idea if someone is found where they shouldn't be," he said.

"Abbey," she said aloud. Then she fought with the quilt as she rushed to the door. It didn't stop her from stealing a quick glance at him. There was a smile in those eyes, something raw and innocent. *Why did she know but didn't at the same time?* There was no time to discuss last night.

Claire left, tugging on her pyjama shorts as soon as she was out of sight, irritated by the slight twist of her knickers wedged with her shorts. *Awkward.*

She stopped. Her door was open. She looked to the left. The bathroom door was open. That meant...*shit.*

Claire tried her best to flatten her hair, even took a quick whiff of her top, knowing it possibly could smell of Zack's cologne from his sheets. But she hadn't time, because Abbey was just exiting the kitchen, cup of orange juice in hand, and dressed in Claire's long, blue jersey top.

"Oh, you're up early. Ha ha, how long you been up?" Claire asked, anxiously rubbing the palms of her hands together and, as a habit, pressing her lips down on top of one another.

Her friend snorted. "It's like *eleven.* I was up about fifteen minutes ago. Where were you? You weren't beside me this morning. And I've just used the bathroom." She sipped some of the juice as she wandered towards the sofa.

"Err, I just got the post," Claire lied.

"How? Unless we have a magical door that I don't know about, I'm pretty sure you're supposed to come from that way." She pointed towards the front door.

Great one, she thought.

As much as she hated Zack's abrupt intrusion, it may have saved her from Abbey's interrogation. Abbey soon shut up. It must have been those tiny baby hairs curling down his forehead, or maybe it was the sight of his chest? The list could go on. *Shut up,* she told herself, refusing to make eye contact with him.

"Morning," he said, wandering towards the

kitchen. Abbey was staring a little harshly, literally pinning her gaze on every inch of him. Claire had to nudge her with her feet. *That wasn't out of jealousy,* she reminded herself.

"So I've spoken to Ryan," Abbey said, a little less interested in Zack as he moved out of her sight. "We spoke on the phone. I think we're good, but we're going to talk through it when I go back this afternoon."

"That's great news. I told you everything would be all right," Claire replied. "We could have a girls' day out, if you want. I need a break from work, and my wardrobe needs updating. How about it?"

"Sure."

Zack returned, holding the carton of orange juice. "Well, it was awfully nice to meet you, Abbey," he said, smiling as he headed towards his bedroom. Abbey blushed, watching as he left the room until he was out of sight.

"Knock it off," Claire hissed, scowling at her friend. "You're not single."

"Well, if I am, I'm so moving in, and I don't care if I live on the freaking couch."

***

ZACK

Zack was feeling a little less optimistic about Project 42 as he added the final touches to the PowerPoint. In approximately two weeks he'd be fighting for its survival, asking the council to think of the housing and energy crises over the other alternative of a shopping centre. He was beginning to think that three months was pointless now. Kyle had only been messing about when he'd suggested this. It was supposed to a week or so, mess about, see what it's like living without Benson funding in his back pocket, and then it turned serious. Project 42 became its purpose, and now he didn't think it stood a chance. So why not just give it two weeks and then return to his old life? Go back to signing business contracts? Go back to having a whollop of money and spending it incessantly?

He sighed, sitting back in the kitchen chair. It had been almost a month. It wasn't any different than his normal, except money, signing over business contracts, and attending meetings. It was the same in the respect of doing nothing. His father didn't want him to expand; his father wanted him to be kept in a pen, following orders, turning a blind eye towards the company's own involvement in corruption, and continually just playing that rich boy. He couldn't entirely blame his character on his father. Zack enjoyed sex, like any other man. But what he hated was being minimised to just that. After all, that previous gala proved his identity as the CEO was non-existent.

And now *Claire.* What on earth was going on there? Last night, there was no interruption, and yet he didn't have sex. It made no sense. Was he becoming a monk? She was right there. *Again.* Wanting him. Nothing was making sense.

***

CLAIRE

"Yeah, that's it. Punch the fuck out of it!" Zack motivated Claire as she jabbed the punching bag he held firmly. Claire threw all her strength at it, even as sweat cascaded down her forehead, and clenching her teeth meant the pain soared.

How on earth she went from browsing clothes to the gym, she didn't know. It was four in the afternoon, and Abbey had left about two hours ago. She was more like her usual self and fitter in mind to drive. The apartment felt empty without her, sadly. Zack had finished his side of the PowerPoint and then, after a few minutes of encouragement, got her along to the gym.

"That's it!" Zack spurred.

"I—swear—Zack," she said through gritted teeth. "Stop—staring—at—my—boobs!" With a final punch, she hit the bag to give herself an immediate break.

Zack chuckled, cuddling his arms around the bag. "I can't help it, love. You're teasing me right now." His gaze roamed the black sports stretchy tank top and three-quarter joggers she wore.

"Pervert," she hissed, picking up her water bottle from off the side. Zack smirked, joining her as she sat down on the matted floor to catch her breath.

"But you feel tons better, don't you?"

Claire nodded. "Although," she paused, taking a sip from her bottle, "I would much prefer I was doing damage to your face rather than the bag."

"How lovely," he said, then he slapped her thigh gently. "Come on. Let's get you on the weights."

Claire whined. "What? The weights? Zack, I need a break...you've had me working for half an hour on that." She jerked her bottle towards the punching bag.

Zack's lips curled agreeably. "Call that exercise, honey? I burn that many calories in sex."

"Shut up, Zack!"

She managed with a slight struggle to get back onto her feet, reluctantly following Zack towards the set of weights. She watched as he placed down his own drink and comfortably lay back on the bench.

"You can spot for me," he told her.

Hesitating for a second, she eventually joined, standing above him so his head was looking up towards her. Then he began to lift the bar off the safety ledges and push the weights up with incredible strength. Claire was not going to lie, but the sheer sight of this gave her goose bumps. Every muscle was working. This was just exactly like something she had read from one of her books—she remembered it was about a personal trainer and client. Only difference was this was real, and that was entrapped in the world of fiction.

"I see your eyes," he said through clenched teeth, midway of lifting the bar up again.

"No, you don't." Then she diverted her eyes elsewhere, tempting herself into a playful mood. "*Ooooh,* look at that fella over there," she whispered.

"What?" He dropped the bar on the ledges and sat up. "Who?"

"Packs a lot of muscle. I wonder what else," she

coyly suggested, observing Zack's face through the corner of her eye.

"*Him?*" He frowned. "You're kidding. You're into body builders?"

The hefty man was lifting weights, ear plugs in, and probably fetishizing about himself and the weights, judging from the affectionate admiration of himself in the opposite wall-sized mirror. There was a lot of muscle. The man looked like the incredible hunk. Of course, that was way too much for her to even consider. He'd probably squash her in bed.

"Oh, yes. I do have a type, you know? Tons of muscular—"

She paused as she observed Zack discreetly checking himself out, scaling the size of himself in muscular mass to the other man.

"Oh, your face!" she laughed.

Zack scowled. "Not funny."

***

ZACK

Zack's brows knitted as she walked off towards the exercise bikes that sat ahead in the middle of the space. He could swear he was becoming more possessive by the minute. Not only was he jealous, but he was near to throwing a punch or two if need be. *For goodness sake*, he thought, *what was seriously going on with that mind of his?*

Claire cycled a little faster as soon as he came over. He moved to the front of the bike, resting his arms onto the handles, hindering Claire's ability to rest her hands on them properly.

"What do you want now?" She sighed.

"I've come to bug you. What else does it look like?" he mumbled, resting his chin into the groove of his folded arms. "So change of plan. I'm kind of self-conscious now, and due to your recent comment, I feel out of place and prefer if we went back home."

"Aw," Claire cooed. "Does Zacky feel hurt that he won't be as strong as those beefy men? Hm?"

"Yeah, maybe you could kiss me better?"

Funny how things changed between them like a turtle on steroids. It didn't seem to matter how much she tried to distance herself or try to tell herself she wasn't interested in Zack; she was a hypocrite. Maybe she just liked his attention? Maybe she wasn't really interested? She begged for anything than confessing otherwise.

"Fat chance. Now move on. I'm actually enjoying myself right now."

Zack pouted. "No kiss?"

"No!" she spat.

He shrugged his shoulders, moving off the bike. "Fine. I'll be over in the corner cowardly crying."

"Yeah, you do that," Claire said.

Her stomach stopped fluttering as soon as he left, as did the wild spastic shivers down her back. If there was one thing she greatly despised, it was Zack's ability to affect her like that. She wondered with curiosity how this attraction would disappear.

Less than twenty minutes later, and when she had the courage to look over to Zack, who was still working on his legs, she was about to give up until a stranger appeared at her side. Usually she was okay with confrontation, but the way he leered at her, it suddenly gave her the utter creeps.

"Can I help you?" she asked as she got off the seat.

"You sure can. How about you give me your number?" the man said, ogling inappropriately at her cleavage and then back up to her face.

Claire shook her head. "No, thank you."

"Why not?"

"Because I said so. Now excuse me," she replied politely, wanting him to move so she could get past. He hung his arm loosely on the bike's handle, grinning with triumph. From the corner of her eye, and the fact the man kept briefly chuckling back towards his friends in the corner of the room, she suspected this was a game of some sort to them.

"Would you move? I've asked you politely, now I'm getting pissed—so move," she snapped, careful to keep her voice down so she wouldn't bring too much attention towards the matter.

"I'll move if you give me your number, baby girl," the man replied, again grinning ear to ear and only further being motivated by the chorus of laughter behind him.

"Move it before I fucking punch you in the face, dickhead," she hissed, her right hand balling into a fist. The man held his hands up, chuckling in defence as if suspecting slight truth in the statement—which to be honest, Claire did mean it.

"Move."

Taking not another chance, the man laughed nervously. "Chill. I was kidding. I'm going. I'm going." Then he quickly scuttled off back towards his group of friends, leaving both Claire and who she suspected butted in, Zack, alone.

"Thanks," she muttered, picking up her water bottle from the holder. "Although I was handling it."

Zack followed Claire towards the exit. "It sure looked like it."

"I was!" she objected. "I could have handled myself."

Zack sighed as he held the glass door open for her. "Claire, stop being so proud and just accept I helped you out there."

She sighed. "Fine...thank you, *again*."

A short escape of breath fled her lips as Zack clasped her arm, pushing her lightly towards a wall. Was it happening again? She expected him to meet her lips—instead, he tenderly kissed her right cheek.

"Is that a pout I see?" he muttered, pulling gently back.

Claire blushed as she denied it, laughing. "Shut up. Go eat a dick."

How more irresistible can he get? she thought, watching as he wetted his bottom lip with a flicker of his tongue. "Let's be honest here, Claire...we all know that isn't what you had in mind."

Claire coyly rolled her head to the side and intentionally began walking her fingers up his torso, stopping at the top of his tank top.

***

ZACK

Zack's train of thought halted, eagerly anticipating what was to come next. With no hesitation, Claire brought her hands to either side of his face, observing how his eyes quivered with exuberance. Leaning in slowly, Zack's insides clenched further with excitement, just like fireworks being setting off inside his stomach. Her lips were inches away from his own, yet remained stationary, allowing her to take control. Without warning, rather than joining lips, Zack felt the hot movement of her tongue gliding up his left cheek.

"Did you just *lick* my cheek?"

"Yes, I did."

"You...sly little fox," he said with a grin.

She was such a hypocrite. Don't like the guy? Not even a bit?

CHAPTER FIFTEEN

CLAIRE

Claire grinned at the unquestionable hunger dilating her pupils at the sight of the chicken nugget approaching her lips. Her stomach had been agreeably growling for the last five minutes, waiting for the arrival of crispy battered chicken. But no more could she wait. The familiar aroma chased through her nostrils, teasing her as if she were a dog salivating on command. Gradually, she opened her mouth, guiding the chicken in until abruptly it was snatched away.

"Hey!" Claire yelled angrily, throwing both hands out.

***

ZACK

Zack roared with laughter, relishing the supreme control he had upon Claire to switch her temper on just like a ticking bomb. He took time to chew the chicken nugget, knowing he was irritating Claire further, and she responded predictably with a gasp.

***

CLAIRE

"You're a fat motherfucker!" she hissed, folding her arms in fury. Seeing the satisfaction on his lips had totally affected her appetite—annoyed with his deliberate action to take first bite, Claire did not feel like eating at all.

Claire felt guilty enough when reluctantly agreeing to order the chicken combo at a fast-food restaurant. They'd just been to the gym. Her stomach growled, *it* growled towards the imbecile that Claire was, for allowing Zack to put her off—so with a quick swipe, she took a chicken nugget from the centre of the table and plopped it in her mouth, knowing she did not want to sacrifice her hunger for him.

"I can't believe I've just wasted burning calories for this," she said, "but it was so worth it."

"So, how was your friend, anyway?" he asked, changing topics.

"She was fine. Although I'm glad she's gone, because I didn't want you to endanger her," she replied, shovelling a handful of fries onto her plate.

Zack frowned lightly. "What did I do?"

"What don't you do?" She rolled her eyes.

There was knock on the front door. Claire got up.

"It seems so much effort to walk. Can't you answer it?" she pleaded.

"You're up. You've pretty much made it already."

Claire sighed, narrowing her eyes at him before making her way out of the kitchen towards the front door. She was certain she wasn't expecting anyone, and there were no services coming out like the plumber, so she had not a clue who it was. It wouldn't be Abbey again. Nor would it be Darren, who couldn't even remember what number she lived at. Was it someone Zack knew, or just some door-to-door salesman looking to flog off cheap products?

She tightened her ponytail before opening the door. She was full of frustration when instantly she was taken aback by Jason standing there with a small bouquet of mixed flowers. "You didn't forget, did you?" Jason joked half-heartedly, raising his right eyebrow up.

"Claire!" Zack yelled from the kitchen. "Who's at the door?"

She pressed her lips briefly together before shouting back in an uncomfortable manner, "J-Just…shut up for one moment. I'll be—" Before shutting up herself, she gaped again at Jason, who stood patiently waiting to be invited in.

"I…went to the gym."

"So I see. You agreed on Friday that I was taking you out at seven?"

"I *did*?" she whispered softly, utterly trying her hardest to recall that part of the day, but everything seemed to revolve around Zack. "Oh, *wait!*" she blurted out. "I did! I mean, of course I did." She felt so embarrassed—both on his behalf and her own. How stupid could she have been? "Shoot...I mean...I just got back. There was—lots of traffic," she added, hoping Jason would buy her lame lie. But come on! It didn't sound legit at all, even as she said it.

Jason nodded slowly. "Okay, that's fine. I'll just wait." He was clearly referring to the living room that sat behind Claire with its sturdy couch and plush cushions.

His polished shoe was inches away from entering when she exclaimed. "No—I mean." She paused to settle her alarmed tone. "Wouldn't it be better if you waited in the car? I'll come out to you."

"Well, these are for you," he said, giving her the flowers.

Claire smiled lightly. "Thank you. They're lovely."

So, was she still going along with this lie? Actually making him believe she's interested just to be stubborn? The evidence was clearly there. She was clearly attracted to Zack. *No,* she told herself. But what about Jason? She didn't fancy him at all.

He stood there for perhaps a second or two, and so did she, uncomfortable with the silence that came after. She was relieved when he turned on the sole of his foot and headed down the corridor. If she felt any sense of achievement, it didn't last very long, as she realised she now had to go along with the date.

Closing the door, she placed the flowers onto the side table, cautious. She wasn't sure she wanted

Zack to see them as she headed back into the kitchen. With some revelation, Zack was washing up this morning's plates and cutlery—something she never expected to see.

"Wow, you're actually doing something to help out?" Claire said, gobsmacked, forgetting her main priority for a moment.

"Yes. Aren't I just handy? Such a husband," he joked, placing a wet dish onto the side. "So did you tell me to shut up because that was your delivery of porn magazines or something?" Zack teased.

Claire rolled her eyes. "Yeah, totally."

"Oh, so it was. I totally understand that you're feeling a little inexperienced in my presence."

Claire sighed. "*Really*?"

"Okay, okay. So, who was it then, *really*?" Zack asked as he dried his hands upon the teal tea towel left on the side counter. Claire hesitated for a second, debating whether to share the truth or brew up a little lie.

"It was Jason," she exhaled. His brows lifted, then fell, but he did not come up with any snarky comments.

"What did he want, or should I say, what does he want?" he muttered, slightly unusual for Zack.

"You know, from Friday—he messaged me," Claire replied, her feet shuffling uncomfortably.

"Oh."

Claire gulped. "S-So—I'm gonna go get changed then. You can still watch a film or TV programme without me. I'll probably be back by nine o'clock."

"Okay."

***

The date wasn't out of the ordinary—a classic meal between two people, a few shared tales and jokes around the table before splitting the bill. She didn't know how much longer she could keep it all up, pretending to be someone she wasn't. She was finding it utterly stupid. What did she have to prove? If she was trying to prove to Zack that she wasn't interested, she was failing. Any idiot could see she was attracted to the man. And here she was, stringing on some poor fella, someone she'd considered a friend, who liked her more than enough for a second date. Claire should stop this before it got all out of hand. Like, *really?* Would she be pretending till they got married, had a child, a house and dog called Rufus? This wasn't right. It was pulling someone down for her own selfish sake.

Jason switched off the engine. He'd just driven them from an Italian restaurant, and now the awkward silence enveloped them. He probably saw it as being bashful, but to Claire, it was a decision between life and death. As dramatic as that sounded, she really did have the opportunity now to set things straight, make Jason aware she wasn't interested, and apologize for leading him on like that. That was the right thing to do. The other alternative was to lie, pretend, and make the guy fall more in love with her than he already was. Claire wished she had a potion, one that could wipe his entire memory of their dates.

"I really enjoyed myself again." He smiled sweetly, resting his hand on the centre joystick. And there was the silence, broken. It was now her turn to answer.

What choice? Be truthful or lie? But why would she lie? It was pretty obvious to Zack. It should be pretty obvious to herself.

"Oh, me too. It was another great catch up," she replied, anxiously looking to her hands in her lap. *Was that all? A subtle hint? Couldn't she just tell him straight?* She was looking outside now, begging herself to just get out.

"Yeah, so, like—"

"Erm, I'm sorry to be rude…" she interrupted. *Now what,* she said to herself. *Just say it! Say you're not interested,* she pleaded inwardly.

"Yes?"

Yes, go on, Claire. Tell him. She could hear Zack prowling about in her head.

She was an idiot. Instead of telling him the truth, she turned in the passenger's seat, leaned over, and connected her lips with his. Somehow, she was trying to tell herself to feel. *Want, need, anything,* that could suggest she was interested in Jason. His soft, thin pink lips, became hungrier, greedier against hers, *hers,* that felt like a blank canvas being manipulated, no control, no nothing. His tongue then pushed through…it felt moist, fighting her own weak and defenceless. Claire hoped snogging him would invest some sort of emotional attachment—instead, it only cruelly led another man on for the sake of her stubbornness.

Claire pulled back. "I have to go."

"I'll see you Monday at work." He smiled, tasting his bottom lip.

She forced a smile as she opened the door and got out. Claire didn't even feel she necessarily needed to wave him off, so she sped a little in her strides towards the apartment door, buzzing in the code to enter. She felt disgusted with herself—this wasn't right. Jason deserved better than a lie.

"Fuck. Fuck. Fuck," she cursed, once she was safely in her kitchen. She kicked off her high heels, pulling out the kitchen chair aggressively as she flopped her head into her hands. *What was the point of the lying?*

"Someone doesn't sound too pleased," Zack said.

She lifted her head from her arms.

"*So,* how did it go?" he asked, insistent as he snatched the adjacent chair and sat down.

"It was fine," she grumbled. "Why do you care?"

"I guess I care because I really don't understand what you're playing at, Claire. Do you?" he replied, sounding frustrated and a little offended.

She shrugged her shoulders.

"I mean, I thought I could be fucked up, but you're really taking the biscuit," he said, running his hand through his hair.

"What do you want me to say, Zack?" she snapped.

"Just what the fuck do you want? What's my part in all of this? You're fucking with another guy, and then you're—I don't even know what's going on between us. I mean…" He got up off his chair, aggressively waving his hand about. "I could have slept with you Friday night. I *wanted* to. It would have been easy—"

"Easy? Really? Now I'm easy, am I?" she cut him off.

"I don't mean it like that. You know what I mean," he argued.

"I don't care what you mean. Just fuck you!" she shouted, getting up off the chair.

"Fuck *me?* Fuck you, Claire," he spat bitterly.

Claire stomped out the kitchen, slamming her bedroom door.

CHAPTER SIXTEEN

CLAIRE

So, maybe she was being more of a dick that night. He had a point. What was his part in all of this? It wasn't right for her lead on Jason. Then, there was the question: was she doing just the same with Zack, and arguably leading him on too? What did she want? If she wanted Zack, why didn't her mind let her? And if she didn't want Jason, why was her mind telling her to lead him on? As much as she hated confessing, she knew every part of Jason's involvement was tangled up with her state of mind surrounding Zack. It just made sense.

She sat in her room all night, hearing the odd door opening, closing, and footsteps across the corridor, but not once a sound of a voice. He was pissed off. She was pissed off. Only hers was questionable.

On the following morning, Claire awoke with reminders of last night—from the hugging of her fitted dress to the eerie silence that lingered about.

Pushing her feet out of the bed, Claire ran her fingers through her bedraggled locks and then rubbed her tired eyes in effort to spur her on for the day ahead. She knew it was not going to be as promising as one could hope, and with the problem of both Zack and Jason, it wasn't going to be easy, either.

Shuffling her feet towards her bedroom door, she counted in her head to ten before turning the handle. Part of her had expected Zack to be waiting there, as sad as that sounded, yet he was not there, nor could she hear the running splutter of water from the shower, and when she headed through the corridor, she took a single peek through his open bedroom door. Zack's duvet was tangled, but there was not a soul to be seen. She could only wonder if he perhaps left early to go to the gym or completely escaped.

How strange it was sitting at the kitchen table drinking coffee on her own. She had gotten used to Zack's morning ritual: his tea or coffee, his cornflakes or just toast, and if he was feeling adventurous, he'd whip up a batch of pancakes. Now, it was just Claire, her dull coffee, and a dry piece of burnt toast.

And then Monday came. Zack hadn't shown his face at all. She finally heard his footsteps around ten o'clock at night. She wanted to talk to him, but she chose the coward's route and remained tucked in her room, where she'd been for the majority of the day.

The journey on the bus felt empty. She'd gotten used to him being there. It was blatantly stupid what they argued over. He had every right to be mad. Maybe it was because he hated being used. It didn't mean he was interested; he was just annoyed that he wasn't solely invested in, even if Claire hadn't wanted to invest those sorts of feelings into Jason. But what about Friday? Had he not stopped them? Maybe he wasn't feeling it, or he had, in fact, heard a noise. But where was the sense in that? Her mind didn't want to admit it, so she turned to look outside, trying to pay attention to the crowds of traffic outside.

Darren sat ahead at the kitchen table, half-asleep and stirring the shit out of his cup of tea as Claire entered. Thankfully neither Jason nor Zack had made an entrance, leaving her some time to clear her mind of guilt. His head lifted slowly, and the edges of his lips curled as Claire approached.

"You look tired," Claire remarked as she took a seat opposite him.

"That's because I am," Darren replied, placing the teaspoon on the side.

"What did you do last night then?" she asked, curious as to why he looked like he just wrestled with the duvet all night.

Darren chuckled after he took a sip. "You wanna know the details, do you?"

"Well, knowing you, it's not going to be clean. Is it?"

"Nope." He smiled. "It certainly isn't. I guess that's what young love is like. I'll leave the details out." He swallowed a mouthful of his tea, gasping as he sat back. "I needed that. So, how was your weekend?"

"Honestly, shit. I had my old roommate around. You remember Abbey, right? I think you met her here and there. Well, she had an argument with her boyfriend. I then went on another date with Jason. And really, I'm being such a shit person because I'm leading him on," she confessed, leaving out the details on Zack.

"Well, shit, Claire," Darren said. "I was expecting something like you had sex with him in the backseat of his car, and you're feeling incredibly sore like a virgin, 'cause we *know* how long it's been for you." He raised his brows in a confronting manner. "So, what are you going to do about Jason? 'Cause I hate to break it you, love, but leading a guy on never goes well, especially one who's cute and adorable like Jason."

"I'm going to have to tell him eventually. I don't know what's wrong with me these days, Darren. I feel sick of myself. I genuinely don't understand," she sighed.

"Is there another guy in all this? Because usually there's two types of leading on: either you're desperate for attention, as in hoe for life, or you don't want to confess your feelings for another," he explained. "Now, I know, honey, that you're not a hoe, but if you ever wanted to be, I will—no matter what—support you. That's all I'm saying."

"Gee—"

"Speak of the devil," he interjected, glaring at Claire.

Carefully, she moved around in her chair, expecting to see Zack, but it was much worse—Jason. Instantly, as weak as she could she be, Claire sunk into her chair and hid her face with the side of her hand, hoping he wouldn't suspect that the brunette sitting in the chair was Claire. But if anyone had common sense around here, they all knew Claire hung out with Darren; it was a running joke in the office of them being twins at one point, for they rarely were seen without the other.

"Hey, Darren," Jason said.

Darren's eyes lit up like a fireworks parade as he replied joyfully, "Jason, good to see you. How was your weekend?"

Claire could feel Jason's smile and eyes burning at the back of her head as he said, "Wonderful. Just wonderful. And yours?"

"Oh, lovely. Was just one of those weekends."

Claire's eyes pinpointed onto Darren's, knowing all too well that he was thoroughly enjoying this and would gleefully take a front row seat with a bag of popcorn for this drama.

"Claire," Jason began, sending prickles of anxiety across her skin. "Could we talk?" he asked. She nodded, slowly getting to her feet, and watched as Darren mouthed encouraging words before pretending to find his empty cup of tea more interesting than whatever was about to occur between herself and Jason.

Rubbing her wrists anxiously together as she followed Jason out of the kitchen, she began to think of ways she could break it down to him. Or rather slowly let him loose from the illusion that they made a great couple together. Either way, she needed to make sure it was well-deserving and wouldn't demoralise the poor man. Jason headed out into the emergency stairwells—a place that Claire was all too familiar with.

His smile broke out immediately, and his hands found her own. "Claire, man. It's been barely a day, and I've already missed you. The other night was just—it was phenomenal, baby. I can call you that, right?" He chuckled with a blush.

Claire's smile was weak as she encouraged a word or two from her mouth. "Yeah—about that."

Jason couldn't even remain patient a second longer—he launched his lips against hers. Claire's eyes opened further in amazement as he deepened the kiss, whereas she instead stood there, longing to hold onto the rails of the stairs for stability. Finally, after another second, he pulled back, smiling with confidence. How was she going to let the guy down now? He had literally just pounced on her vulnerable lips there and then, just like a loitering fly quickly snapped in by a hungry spider.

"J-Jason. I—"

"No, don't say anything," Jason interrupted, pressing his forefinger against her lips. "You can tell me how amazing I am over a coffee at lunch, okay? Gosh, this feeling you're giving me is breathtaking." He pecked her cheek, then smiled as he headed out the door. It would have been hysterical from an outsider's view: a grown-ass man acting like a love-sick teenager. It was more hysterical on Claire's character. She wasn't normally ever bashful. Claire knew she was the kind of woman to tell a person straight, and now here she was, completely going against what was morally right, and who she was. Had someone stole her identity?

Claire gaped. *Did that just happen? Did he just kiss me?* Could she say she allowed that to happen just then? *Well,* to be honest, no, because it was an absolute surprise.

Claire sluggishly trailed towards her cubicle, where an eagerly anticipating Darren sat in her chair, biting at the end of his blue pen. He got up, gesturing that she take her seat. Claire slowly sat down, blinking several times to adjust to the fact that what just happened, happened.

"I gotta say," Darren blurted. "For a man who got let down, he sure looks happy. You sure the guy even wanted to date you?"

Claire remained staring into space as she muttered, "I barely managed a word."

Darren snapped his fingers. "Claire! Over here. Not over there. What do you mean?"

She blinked this time with full awareness of her surrounding as she replied, "He kissed the living daylights out of me—I didn't even get to tell the guy. And he practically shut me up to tell me we're having coffee together at lunch."

The sheer sound of Darren's laughter cut through the office. "What? Oh my goodness! That's hilarious!" Darren cackled, throwing his hands onto the desk.

Claire frowned. "No, it's not! Darren, how am I supposed to let him down now? He thinks I liked that—it's all my fault!"

Darren's wipe of his tears was very theatrical. "Oh, Claire," he cried, "this is just so good. Come on. You've practically sealed your wedding vows to the guy. Heck, you'll have two little kids called Joey and Carys running around!"

"Shut up! This isn't funny, Darren," she hissed. "I need some air." She stood up.

Claire picked up her bag and headed for the lifts when Graves suddenly intervened, snapping his fingers to draw her attention. She stopped, fearing he was catching her out on Darren's parade over there or to discuss why she was leaving at this hour when she knew herself she hadn't even started work.

"Claire," he exhaled, "I was looking for you. Could you do me a favour?"

What a relief, she thought as she nodded in response. Another time she might have thought about strangling the man with the amount of work he toppled onto her. "Could you deliver this to the CEO personally? I haven't got time to go up there, and my email has crashed. It's just paperwork for Project 76. All you need to do is deliver this to his PA," he explained, handing her the manila folder. "It shouldn't be too much of a hassle."

Claire reluctantly took it. She would have done twenty thousand sit-ups just to get herself out of that sticky situation. She'd had enough of listening to Jason.

Graves rushed off, holding his lanyard aggressively as he headed towards the men's bathroom directly adjacent the two sets of lifts. She held onto the folder as she called for the lift, hoping it would hurry as she spotted Jason walking about, snaking in the maze of cubicles.

***

ZACK

Zack was signing a contract, renewing Benson's partnership with manufacturers that supplied the company building materials for its contractors. Olivia popped her head around the door jamb at that moment.

"Sir, I have Claire Winter here. She's got some paperwork from the Sales and Marketing department. IT staff are working on the department manager's email server," she reported, the frames of her glasses a little further down her small nose.

Zack clenched his stomach. "Just take them off her—"

Olivia's phone began to ring. "Oh, I'm sorry, sir. I need to take this," she interjected, bringing the phone to her ear. "I'll tell her to bring them in," she added, disappearing from sight.

What was he supposed to do? He couldn't let her see him. He quickly sat down, turned his chair to face the huge standing windows, and prayed to God she wouldn't recognise him. There was some scuttling of his feet as he attempted to get comfortable. Why he was bothering to play this anymore, he didn't know. He'd proven to Kyle pretty much the project itself might as well be scrapped, and their relationship was dwindling.

The door opened.

"Erm, Mr. Benson, I deeply apologise. Mr. Graves would have sent these earlier, but his email server appears to be down. Instead, he's offered paper copies of last month's marketing costs," she said politely.

Zack didn't utter a word.

"W-Where would you like me to put them?" she asked, breaking that dead silence. She was probably already getting the image of a disagreeable man from how impolitely he had his chair turned away. The chair's tall back covered the back of his head, so in reality, she was talking to the back of a chair rather than a man.

He was shaking in his bones now. Zack shifted in the chair slightly, knocking something over, only becoming aware that it was a bottle of water that had flipped off the left-hand side of the desk.

"I'll get it for you," she offered.

Zack snapped. "No! Leave it. Just leave the work on the desk and go." He held his breath, hoping his voice wouldn't give him away. There was a pause or two before he finally heard her place the paperwork on the desk and bid goodbye as she exited the room. He exhaled, slouching in the chair as he undid his sleeves.

***

CLAIRE

Claire turned on her heel, feeling a little offended over the poor respect she'd received off the man. His tone was fiercely aggressive, like a lion unable to be tamed. Why couldn't he face her? Was the man that vain he couldn't speak face to face with his employee? Claire didn't even want to spare a second thought as she closed the door behind her, passed his PA, who was speaking on the phone, and headed towards the lift. *Well, he was a jerk,* she thought as she entered the metal four-by-four shaft.

She was on her floor in less than a couple of minutes after stopping at six different floors, shuffling aside to allow people in, but *finally,* she was able to scoot from the lift and settle back to her cubicle. It was barely ten o'clock, and there was still no sight of Zack. They were done with their presentation, so she didn't have to worry about nagging him, but it still didn't settle her nerves. *Great,* she sighed aloud. That's all she needed. Claire was just hoping he'd show up by now. It didn't exactly reflect good on him, *not that she cared,* she told herself. *Maybe it would be easier if he just got dismissed.*

Claire opened up last month's spreadsheet, preparing herself as she fought to find the energy to speak on the phone with the clients.

"*Hello,* Benson's Corporation—"

It had been hectic, not that she expected anything less. There were times she wanted to curl up into a ball and cry, but she couldn't. She was on the phone. She was a representative of the company. At twelve and still no sign of Zack, she logged off temporarily, readying herself for the next crisis. She remembered this morning's disaster with Jason. A coffee date. It took effort as she sluggishly got up and pulled her handbag across her shoulder, and it took more effort to attempt a smile as she spotted Jason waiting for her at the lifts. Claire hoped she would regain her confidence this afternoon and set him straight, but from the way he walked up to her and pecked her right cheek, she was feeling more anxious about that possibility.

"Let's grab that coffee then," he said, clasping his hands together, briefly rubbing his palms together before fisting them into his pockets. Claire bit on her tongue as she headed into the lift, shuffling to the side, thankful they weren't the only ones in here.

Jason had no intention of going to the canteen; he insisted they walk across the road towards the small coffee shop on the corner. Claire had always thought of Bees as expensive: sandwiches could cost up to three pounds, and their tea was an extra pound. But the more insistent she was, the more persistent he'd be, so they ended up at the coffee shop, sitting in a couple chairs in the back of the shop. The aroma was thick with churning coffee beans, highlighting Claire's need for energy.

So far, he was busy ordering their food, giving her the time to sink back into the chair and relax whilst she could. It didn't work. She felt as stiff as a pole. She looked around, wishing she could have been that person with the blue beanie typing on his laptop or that woman munching on her sandwich. Anything that meant she could get herself out of this situation.

Jason soon returned, carrying a cardboard drinks tray in one hand, and the other was pinching the edges of the sandwich cartons. He plopped them down. "And *heeere* we go. One Americano, and a latte, no sugar, for the lady," he said, then picking out a packet of crisps he'd stashed in his coat pockets and throwing them lightly onto the table.

"So." He sat down. "How was your morning?"

"Erm, good. Just catching up with the log book for a client. You?" she replied, thanking him as he passed the latte.

He smiled, staring straight at her. It was starting to make her feel self-conscious as he sat there saying nothing. Claire couldn't say it. She went to open her mouth. "So, uh—"

"You know," he muttered, cutting her off, then licking his bottom lip, "I just couldn't stop thinking about you, if I'm honest."

She cringed inside. *Fuck, fuck.* She had to come clean. There was no way she was gonna keep this up, and besides, what was there for her to prove? Zack wasn't here for her to pretend she liked him, and what difference would it make knowing she had her tongue down Zack's throat, anyway?

"Jason—"

"Before you say anything, I just want to say our dates have been amazing. I don't want to rush you into anything, but when the time is right, I'd really like to give us a shot, you know?" he interjected, once again forcing her to close her mouth.

Claire was getting fed up now.

"Erm," she began, "yeah, it's too early at the moment." She looked down to her cup, unaware she was scratching the sides off, causing the papery surface to disintegrate into tiny pieces. Why couldn't she just say the truth? This wasn't Claire. Claire was confident. She told people straight, and now she was slowly becoming smaller and smaller by the second.

"Oh, of course, but you would consider it, right?" he asked. He sounded a little hurt. It was making her feel guiltier by the second.

"Oh, oh, yeah, I mean, let's just see how things go," she replied. "I'm still getting to know you. You know what I mean?"

Jason agreed, but he didn't sound exactly too pleased. *But would you?* she asked herself. She was playing the guy. At first, it was motive for Zack's surprise appearance. And now? What was the purpose? She wished she had listened to Darren, maybe declined what she thought was a friendly outing, but what would that have done? Claire wasn't to have known. *And what Claire could have done is come clean*, she told herself.

The conversation didn't seem to flow or go anywhere. Jason spoke a little about work, some past events, and very soon, they were making their way to the department floor. She was glad, even if the relief was temporary. Claire said goodbye and side-stepped awkwardly, catching the hint as he attempted to peck her cheek.

"Er, I'll text you," she said, then scuttled away like the tide rolling out.

Darren was already at his cubicle typing away…she decided it was her turn to shuffle over to his. He looked up, taking out his earplugs as he smiled. "Zack's back," he said, immediately ensnaring her full attention.

"Where?" she demanded, looking around the office but failing to see a single face over the towering cubicle blocks. *Genius,* she thought.

"He's at that desk Graves found him. He came in

229

abouuuuuut…" He clucked the top of the roof of his mouth. "About twenty-five minutes ago. I think I saw him with Monica."

"Oh."

"Well, did you come clean? Does Jason know?" he asked, leaning his elbow on the side as he turned to the left.

"I mean, I—no," she sighed, running her fingers through her hair. "I couldn't even find the energy to tell him. He wants to go official and all. I've messed up big time, Darren."

"Tut, tut, Claire. This isn't gonna exactly put you in a good position if you don't tell him," he explained, flicking a piece of loose cotton off his light blue shirt.

"I knoooow," she grumbled, sighing as she leaned against the cubicle wall. "Can't you just tell him?"

"Honey, you're a big girl now. Ain't none of that bullshit. I mean, what am I supposed to say? Claire, you've got to tell him, and more importantly, you just need to admit that there's something going on between you and your roommate."

Claire leaned up. "What? No, pssf. There isn't. Trust me."

"*Right,* so you didn't just eagerly start looking around for him when I told you he was here?" He crossed his arms.

"I-I was just—I mean, I just wanted to know if he was all right and—" She raised her left shoulder as she tried a convincing honest face. "I have work to give him."

"*Sure.*"

"You know what? To prove it to you, I'm going to walk right over to him and give him that work," she said, raising her head confidently.

"*Sure,* keep denying it," he called out after her as she stomped around to her cubicle.

Claire paused as she watched Zack passing the front of the office, heading for the stockroom. It was like her feet were controlling her then, because she found them hot on his trail, and *fast.* She opened the door; he was at the back reaching for a stack of paper, oblivious that she had just entered.

She cleared her throat.

He turned, and like that, like thunder piercing through the high heavens, the above light glorified that charming face, tempting her to bow down to her knees towards the godlike creature that he was. She swallowed, however, wondering why he hadn't said a word.

With the impending silence on her shoulders, she decided to make the first move. "*So,* where were you this morning?" she asked, looking elsewhere than his eyes.

"Out," he replied dully.

"Well, you could have let me know."

"I didn't realise I had to let you know where I was twenty-four hours of the day. I suppose that isn't enough information for you, though, is it?" He cocked his head to the side, the stack of paper still in his hands. He continued before she had the chance to reply. "Does having sex count?"

"What?" Her face scrunched up with disgust. "You—what's that—I mean, you can't have ditched this morning—"

"No," he calmly interrupted. "I had sex just a few minutes ago. Monica—that's her name, right?"

"You're lying," she hissed. "Why are you being such a jerk?"

"Last I checked, you were the one jerking Jason off," he replied, planning to slip aside and head towards the door.

"Er, fuck you," she snapped, holding his arm. "You're not going anywhere."

He raised his left brow. "I'm not?"

"No. We're sorting out this shit now."

She slowly let loose of his arm, anticipating that he'd stay, considering she was willing to sort, or at least mend what was said Saturday. "Just—just let's sort this out," she reiterated once more.

"I'm listening."

"Now, I think you should apologise about Saturday. You clearly overreacted—"

"I should apologise?"

She crossed her arms defensively. "Yes!"

Zack laughed bitterly. "Oh, that's rich! I should be apologising? I'm not the one prancing about, kissing one guy here and another there, and then when it comes to it, completely denying that you've got feelings for me."

Claire narrowed her eyes. "I do not have feelings for you, Zack. The only feeling I have for you is hate. H-A-T-E. Hate! Do you need me to spell that out for you again?"

"Go ahead, *baby*, spell it out loud and clear!" Zack growled, throwing his hands viciously into the air.

"I hate you!" she shouted.

"Good, 'cause I hate you!" he roared.

It went dead silent. It became a face off. Claire in the one corner, Zack in the other. At any rate, they could clash. She was looking him dead in the eyes, so vexed she didn't know what else she was feeling, but all she could imagine was kicking him to space. He was like this little bug, always finding its way into a house.

"You know, you're—" she began.

"Just shut up," he cut in, dropping the stack of paper on the floor as he closed the gap between them. His lips collided with hers. It was like a wild forest fire had set alight that Claire could no longer refuse. Her fingers glided through his hair as she felt him deepen the kiss, and lustfully, she clung closer to him, wanting every inch of him as close as possible to her own body. It was an old hunger. Zack's tongue invaded her own.

He lifted her up, and she welcomed it by wrapping her legs around his waist as he pushed her up against the stockroom door. Not a word was spoken in return as he began to unbutton the first few buttons of her cream blouse to finally expose her breasts. She was thankful that she wore something a little more tasteful, a brown lace flowered bra. She felt goose bumps all over, and a sheer attack of butterflies swarmed her stomach when his lips caressed her breasts before teasingly her hardened nipples through the flimsy material. Slowly, Zack began to move his lips down; that triggered her stomach to quiver in delight. Nor did he stop when he passed her belly button and intentionally took his time to poke his fingers through either side of her skirt's waistband. Claire grabbed the collar of his shirt in impatience, tugging it in torment.

Gently, he kissed her stomach, then stood up, watching the hunger in Claire's eye hesitate a little before it burned ferociously when he joined their lips and squeezed one of her breasts.

They froze when the door handle moved. Zack instantly locked the door. Claire hurriedly began to fasten her buttons, but she was so shaken that Zack had to take over and finish the job for her.

"Hello? Is somebody in there?"

Claire refused to meet Zack's eyes as she flattened her shirt. She began to do the same to her hair, instantly falling to her knees as Zack opened the door. She began to collect the scattered paper, pretending shit didn't just happen then.

"Sorry." She could see from the corner of her eye Zack shaking a hand. "I must have locked the door. We dropped the paper. I'll go see if there's any more needed in the printer." Then he slid out of sight.

Claire picked up as much as she could, then hurried past her colleague, not breathing a word as she exited the stockroom, sucking in a mouthful of air.

Darren was typing rapidly across the keyboard as Claire returned, heading over to his side of the cubicle. "Where have you been? The stockroom? I thought you flew around the world eighty times," he said.

Claire blinked. "I had to go...get paper."

"Honey, you're flushed. You been having a good

ol' workout in there," Darren jokingly said.

"No, I just couldn't reach the top shelf," she lied.

"Well, in better news, I'm planning drinks and a home-cooked meal at mine tonight. Jonas is coming. I want you to meet him," Darren said, smiling from ear to ear.

Claire's brows raised. "Dinner?"

"Yes, as in sitting around what you call a table and eating what we call food, Claire. *Of course*, a dinner."

Claire scoffed. "Darren, I'm not thick."

"Well, what do you say? We were having dinner over mine anyway, but I kindly suggested that perhaps you'd like to come. That way we can all dine together and finally meet," Darren explained, tapping his pen lightly onto the desktop.

"Of course I would!" She smiled. *Anything to stay away from Zack for the time being,* she thought.

"Great," Darren said. "Mine at seven."

***

ZACK

Claire. Moments ago, he just enjoyed the fucking hottest action in his life. And it seemed to never get old. It was like a cycle: on one hand they fought like cats and dogs, and on the other, they gave each other mouth-to-mouth resuscitation. It just didn't make sense. *What does this all mean, though?* he thought.

"Zack," Monica purred beside him, caressing her

fingers across his hand that was resting on his right thigh. Ever since he'd slept twice with her, she'd become irritating. She had joined him when Graves had assigned Monica to help him with a case study to get him further on track after his mentoring with Claire had finished, but she was no actual help.

"What's up?" Zack asked, gently removing her hand from his thigh, hoping she would get the message. Monica, however, only accepted this as a little "hard to get" move and instead fought back, intentionally moving her hand towards his dick.

"Monica, sweetie," he muttered, stopping her hand from grabbing his manhood under the desk. "Can you relax? I can see you're horny, but can't you give a guy a break?"

"Why, though? We…could go that—"

"Ssssh," Zack interrupted. "Just relax."

Monica hissed. "You weren't like that earlier. You let my hands roam all over you. So, what's changed?" She narrowed her eyes.

Zack groaned. "Monica, I'm not in the mood right now. Get it?"

"*Fine*. I'm going back to my office anyway. I'll speak to you tomorrow."

Chapter Seventeen

CLAIRE

Claire was going to stand her ground. But no. Instead, she was deceived by those god-gorgeous looks, and next thing she knew, she was making out with the guy and gladly throwing her knickers at him. *Yeah, well done, Claire. Great job!* Maybe Zack was right. Maybe she was stubborn. But admitting her feelings for him was like diving into the deep blue sea where hungry sharks circled. It was a disaster waiting to happen.

She tried to interact as little as possible with Zack, refusing to speak about their entanglement, and was out the door in no time, heading for her friend's apartment. That conversation was for another time.

Darren's apartment was situated a few minutes away from a local supermarket and overlooked the car park of the telephone market enterprise, EMEs. Claire resented how he sat on the eleventh floor—it was tiring for her feet when the flat's lifts weren't in working order, and that was most of the time. With little grace, Claire heaved like an aging man, unable to walk more than three steps at a time as she climbed up onto the final step. *Yes, today the lifts decided not to function. Typical.* Brushing her slightly sweaty hands down her freely wrinkled green shirt dress, Claire inhaled. Right, next step, get to Darren's door without collapsing in exhaustion.

He must have been waiting behind the other side of the door, because as soon as she arrived, he opened it with enthusiasm. "Claire, you made it. And darling, you're looking a little red-faced. Lifts not working again?"

"No shit, Sherlock," Claire said jokingly before engulfing his broad torso in her arms.

As Darren pulled back, Claire noticed a male from over Darren's shoulder standing behind him, sheepishly smiling at her. Darren instantly introduced the very attractive man. His blond hair seemed to be kissed by the sun itself, and he had an adorable smile accompanied by dimples.

"And this, Claire, is my super-hot boyfriend, Jonas," Darren introduced, extending his right hand that interlocked with Jonas' welcoming one.

"Nice to meet you." Jonas smiled, using his free hand to shake Claire's.

"And you. I must say, Jonas, I agree with Darren on that—you're mighty handsome!"

Jonas laughed.

"Well, don't just stand there. Get your arse in, Claire. My food ain't being burned because of your tardiness," Darren demanded.

"Yes, sir," Claire said, saluting her hand up a little as she entered the apartment.

Darren's apartment was its usual clean and tidy self. It was also decorated with his famous collection of celebrities' signatures in frames upon the walls. And he took much pride in them knowing the amount of effort he had to make, just so he could bargain the celebrity to sign. There was the story where he hassled Emma Stone's bodyguard, confused the guy by doing the ol' trick of faking that someone in the hotel had broken their leg, and then swooped to Emma Stone like Prince Charming. She was indeed friendly enough to offer her signature before supplying him a quick exit. The good times abroad he had seeking out the celebrities in LA.

"Okay, so you two get chatting whilst I get the drinks." Darren gleamed, excitedly springing towards the small kitchen.

Claire rolled her eyes playfully. "Jonas, I don't know how you're going to handle that one. He's always on his toes."

Jonas chuckled. "I say that to myself every time I see the man." Darren returned to the side of the sofa, holding three wine glasses on a tray. Jonas wasted no time in slipping his arm around Darren's waist. Scooting onto the sofa's arm, Darren nestled comfortably closer into Jonas as he placed the tray onto the coffee table. "But he knows that he ain't be leaving me 'cause he knows where I keep my pistol."

Jonas slapped Darren's knee. "Shut up! You're such an ass."

Claire smiled at their affection and couldn't help at that second to think of Zack. *Wait. What?* Discouraging any more thoughts of Zack, she asked with haste, so much that her tone sounded a little too high-pitched, "So, Jonas, how did you meet Darren? I've heard Darren's side of the story, but we all know he can be a little over-dramatic."

Darren scowled. "Er, excuse me, Claire Winter. But I'll have you know that every word was true. Right, babe?"

Jonas laughed. "Sure, whatever you say."

Darren frowned, getting up to his feet as he began filling the empty glasses with the red wine that sat in the middle of the glass coffee table.

Jonas smiled. "I'm sure you've been told that we met because we lived right next door to each other, and it was due to the occurrence of me getting locked out. There's no question to that, but did Darren tell you the part where he nearly hassled the elderly lady who lives four doors down because of me?"

Claire opened her eyes in bewilderment. "What? You've got to share this!"

Darren gasped. "What! Jonas, don't you dare. That woman still keeps giving me the stares every time I pass her door. And I swear she's got a pair of binoculars up her skirt, because she's always looking from that window whenever I'm just returning home."

Jonas shook his head. "Trust me. It was hilarious."

"What did he do?"

Jonas leaned forward, pressing his arms onto the

ends of his knees as he spoke. "So, basically, I was playing a little hard to get, if you know what I mean?" Then he wiggled his eyebrows. "And before we officially got interested in pursuing this relationship further, I dared…him to sing for me."

"What!" Claire laughed, gasping for air. "Darren can't belt a tune! You should have heard him at last year's work party on the karaoke machine. Let's just say Bieber wouldn't have been impressed."

"I know! I know!" Jonas howled. "Oh, but seriously, you should have been here. I got Darren to sing outside my door and—"

"I'm seriously going to curl up on my bed and cry in a minute," Darren interrupted, shaking his head with embarrassment.

"Babe, you remember what you sang, right?" Jonas sneered.

"Nope. Nope. Nope."

Jonas turned back to Claire as he continued. "So, I got him to sing, right? And I was listening on the other side—well, laughing. But anyway, he stops, and that's when I hear the old lady complaining to Darren for fucking singing. She said it was like her fucking cats meowing when they're disturbed. Or when she'd got fucking diarrhoea! So, Darren was in a war with the old bird, telling her to mind her own business. Oh, it was so funny! She was so brutal with her insults." Jonas was convulsed with laughter, making Darren glower.

Claire was cracking up too, unable to believe it all.

Darren took a sip from his wine, then muttered, "Oh, what is this? Pick on Darren Day? You two—I

241

knew I should have never introduced you. You're a tag team."

"Oh, lighten up, babe," Jonas said, getting up to his feet, then affectionately pecking Darren's cheek. "You're funny, that's all. But hey, I asked you out after that, didn't I?"

Darren's cheeks couldn't even suppress the lifting smile that infected his lips. "Oh, shut up, you!"

Dinner was soon in full swing. Claire couldn't even remember the amount of glasses she had drank listening attentively to Jonas speak on their current affairs. For a couple who had been only dating a week and a half now, there was plenty to share. So much that Claire hated being single. Where were her pillow wars? Or the practical jokes? Oh, these two were just perfect for each other. She could see that too, the way Darren would discreetly caress his fingers on Jonas' hand or even the single glances he would give and receive in return. That was love. And it picked up on the subject of Jason—making her feel much guiltier. She knew it just as well, that there was no way she could deceive a man into believing she was in love with him. There was no way—she couldn't lie to him nor her heart.

* * *

After a few more drinks and a game of Cluedo, Claire was just about ready to go home. Although there was a slight problem, she might have drunk a little too much. The room around her appeared to swirl, and Darren's face became rather distorted until she wasn't even sure if it was him.

"*Man! Woooo! I'm fucked!*" Claire yelled, twirling around on her toes and thrashing the vodka bottle they brought out earlier on, up into the air.

"You're pissed." Darren laughed. "You're not going home tonight."

Claire hiccupped as she dropped the bottle onto the sofa. "No—I'm okay...wooooo! Look at that handsome face." She cupped Jonas' cheeks.

"Claire." Darren scowled. "You're not going back on the bus tonight. You're pissed as fuck."

"You're not my mother, Darren! I'm sure Zack will rescue me. WOOOO!" Claire wailed, pouncing about on her feet. "He's so strong...fucking—"

Darren lifted his eyebrows at Jonas. "I thought she didn't like the guy," he muttered.

Claire collapsed onto the couch, thrusting her hands up as she grumbled. "Take me home. I want home—"

"I don't mind taking her home. I haven't had much. Two glasses at best," Jonas offered, swinging his car keys out of his pocket.

Darren pressed his lips together, observing the state Claire was in. "I don't know. She doesn't seem in a very good state to even walk. And especially all those stairs."

"We'll help her. And I'll drop her off. You know her address, and then—perhaps you know...we can?" Jonas hinted, caressing his fingers gently across the surface of Darren's cheek.

Darren smirked. "You're so evil. Fine. But you get your ass back here as soon as possible or I'm going to bed."

With a lot of difficulty and a few pauses, they both managed to support Claire downstairs, holding each of her arms and pulling her up when her legs felt they were going to give way.

Jonas kissed his boyfriend's lips before getting into the driver's side of the mini four-seater he owned. Claire could barely keep her eyes open and leaned her head uncomfortably onto the seatbelt, feeling the weight of her head drag her down.

"You make sure she gets in all right," Darren told Jonas. "And tell her roommate she'll have a pretty bad hangover in the morning. I'll be surprised if she's in work tomorrow."

"Okay, babe," Jonas replied, switching on the engine.

With every passing streetlight, Claire could only scrunch her eyes further, feeling its intensity increase. Even the sound of the radio playing in the background was like a hurricane ripping a house's roof off. Her head pounded, and her stomach felt sickened to the point where she wasn't sure she could keep it all in. Fresh air blew in from the window onto her face, offering her some relief, but nothing until she could puke up her guts then sleep until morning light. Heck, she couldn't even recall the reason why she drank so much or why she continued to do so despite knowing she had work tomorrow. She must have been so embarrassing moments ago.

"Jonas?" she muttered.

"Yes?"

"I'm sorry if I drank...a little too much. I hardly do this, but..." She hiccupped. "This man I really like is making all my thoughts go dizzy. I rarely know what I'm doing these days," she admitted. "I really like him…" Then soon the drift of sleep fell upon her, so that when she next awakened, she was no longer in the car alongside Jonas and instead was somewhere familiar.

Instead of the uncomfortable seatbelt digging into her neck and the blaring streetlights torturing her tired eyes, she felt the comfort of two bulky arms around her and a layer of some sort upon her. Claire opened her eyes, turning to the figure, and instantly acknowledged it as Zack. She could tell by the contour of his body and the ruthless scent that always lingered in her nostrils.

As exhausted as she was, she muttered. "Did Jonas get back all right?"

There was a pause until she heard Zack reply. "Yeah, he's fine. Called an hour ago. You vomited nearly in your wardrobe, and you tried sleeping on the toilet bowl, but you're in your bed now."

"Zack?"

"What?"

"I'm sorry we argued. Can…you just hold me all night?" she mumbled.

Zack hesitated. "Don't worry about that."

Claire snuggled her arms closer around his torso, too exhausted to reply, and barely able to remember what she said.

***

"Here. Drink this and have two tablets," he instructed as he passed over the box of paracetamol.

245

"Thanks," she muttered, taking a sip from the fresh glass of water. Gosh, how her throat needed that. It felt like a desert moments ago.

"Looks like they won't be expecting you at work today then," Zack remarked as he watched her plop two tablets onto her tongue, then swallow a huge gulp of water.

"Shit," she cursed under her breath, feeling more pathetic for getting herself pissed last night and denying herself any ability to get up this morning and venture off to work. Heck, she couldn't even find a reasonable excuse on why she drank so much.

"Don't worry, I've called you in sick," Zack said, "and I'll be taking the day off too. You need someone to look after your sorry ass." He took the glass from her hands and settled it back on the bedside table.

"Eurrgh," Claire groaned. "I'd rather be left alone than have you looking after me. And besides, I think I know how to deal with a hangover, so just go on. Get your ass to work. I'll look after my sorry ass, thank you very much."

"Not gonna happen, sweetheart," Zack replied. "Now, don't tell me you're gonna lounge about in bed all day? First—I'd say you need a shower, then to brush your teeth."

"Fuck off, Zack," she hissed, snaking back into her quilts. "You're not my mom, dickhead."

"Yet I'm the man who has probably saved your ass from getting a disciplinary warning, don't you agree?" he said, sneering at her. It was irritating her. How he stood there, a grin plastered on his face from cheek to cheek, acting as if he had the higher moral ground.

She couldn't deny that he was somewhat of a help calling in, but that didn't mean she was pleased. Last night felt like a distant memory, yesterday couldn't have been more problematic, and here Zack was, nursing her as if she just broken her foot. There were a few things they needed to go through, and she knew that.

Zack sat down on the edge of her bed, pulling out his phone.

She remained quiet. This hangover didn't even compare to half of what she was feeling. Everything was just piling up on her shoulders. Whatever was going on between herself and Zack, she needed to sort it. The case with Jason. Work. *Everything.*

"You're not seriously staying here all day looking after me, are you?" she asked, defensively pulling the quilt closer to her lap.

Zack looked up from his phone. "For now, yes."

"Even after the shit we've argued about," she hinted, "we—haven't really talked about *that.*" *What have we really talked about?* she asked herself then. She'd only dismissed the question and then tried to shift the blame completely onto him, acting as if his reaction was unnecessary. How could she blame the guy? As far as she knew he saw it, he wasn't deceiving anyone. She *was.*

Zack exhaled gently. "Claire," he paused. Her phone buzzed on the left bedside table. She looked at it, picked it up, and swallowed. *Jason.* "Even if I wanted to. What's there to talk about, *really?*" His eyes flicked to her phone. He must have sensed it was *him,* or he must have caught a glimpse of the several other notifications on her phone received from the exact same person sent earlier this day.

"I-I—"

"Just get some rest. Sleep it off and drink plenty. I'll be around most of the morning, but then I'm out later. I've got some errands to run," he replied, standing up and sliding his phone into his pocket. Zack didn't stand there much longer, soon moving towards her bedroom door and leaving her alone with her thoughts.

Claire sighed, throwing her phone she hadn't realised she was clenching onto the floor.

What was she so afraid of?

Acknowledgements

Thank you to Limitless Publishing for enabling this book to come to life. My editor, Toni, who has supported me endlessly through the ups and downs.

I thank my loving parents who've never stopped believing in me since day one, pushed me to do things I thought were never possible and who continue to support me. I thank my family, my grandparents who offer their unconditional support. My best friend Daniella, who's always been there, proud of me for chasing my dreams. Without them, the possibility of this book being published would be slim. They give me confidence to push myself to do things I would never attempt otherwise.

I'd like to thank Wattpad, from where it all begun and where I'll continue to grow and learn as a writer. I thank my readers from there, who without, this wouldn't be possible. I thank them for their votes, comments and support. They made me more than anything, believe in myself when my confidence slipped.

I thank you, those who've helped, inspired and made the possibility of this book, possible.

Thank you as I continue to learn, grow as a writer.

About the Author

Romance is just one thing J.S.Badham cannot get enough of! Whether it's the typical cliché love-at-first-sight or I-hate-you-but-also-love-you compelling stories, they're always close to her heart! Most will probably see it as trash literature but love is what makes the world go around! So, why not romance?

Her spark for writing began at the age of fifteen; a passion ignited thanks to her favourite author, Rachel Caine (Morganville Vampires) encouraging her that writing is the ability to be able to share inner stories and connect to the world.

J.S. Badham's journey began on Wattpad, her path continues to grow, she continues to learn hoping that some day she'll share a story that is inspiring.

Facebook:
https://www.facebook.com/JSBadham-146220769420998/

Twitter:
https://twitter.com/JSBADHAM1

Wattpad:
https://www.wattpad.com/user/Vampirefangsrules

Instagram:
https://www.instagram.com/j.s.badham/